THE CONJURER

AND OTHER

AZOREAN TALES

DARRELL KASTIN

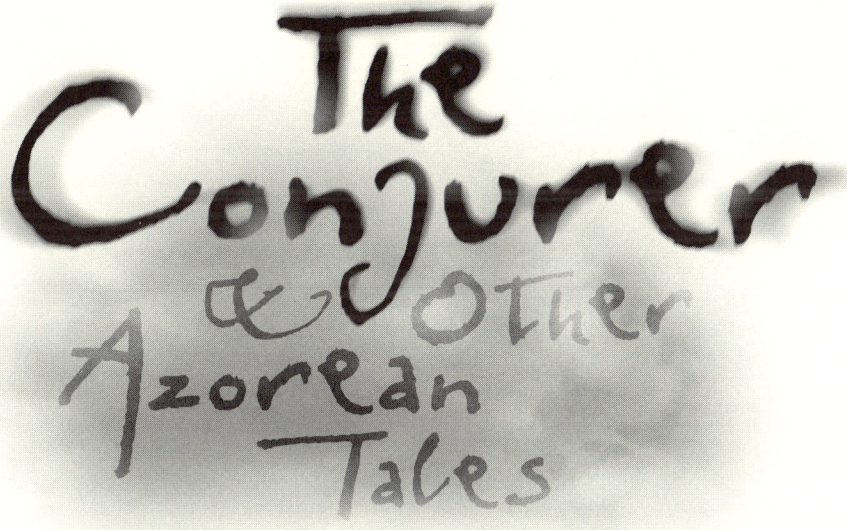

Tagus Press ~ UMass Dartmouth
Dartmouth, Massachusetts

PORTUGUESE IN THE AMERICAS SERIES 19

Tagus Press at UMass Dartmouth
www.portstudies.umassd.edu
© 2012 Darrell Kastin
All rights reserved
Manufactured in the
United States of America
General Editor: Frank F. Sousa
Managing Editor: Mario Pereira
Copyedited by Peter Fong
Designed by Mindy Basinger Hill
Typeset in 10/14.5 Calluna

Tagus Press books are produced and distributed for Tagus Press by University Press of New England, which is a member of the Green Press Initiative. The paper used in this book meets their minimum requirement for recycled paper.

For all inquiries, please contact:
Tagus Press at UMass Dartmouth
Center for Portuguese Studies and Culture
285 Old Westport Road
North Dartmouth MA 02747-2300
Tel. 508-999-8255
Fax 508-999-9272
www.portstudies.umassd.edu

The author would like to thank the editors of the following magazines and journals, in which some of these stories first appeared: *Berkeley Fiction Review*; *Blue Mesa Review*; *Crescent Review*; *Gávea-Brown: A Bilingual Journal of Portuguese-American Letters and Studies*; *Magic Realism*; *Margin: Exploring Magical Realism*; *NEO Magazine*; *Seattle Review*; and *Sulphur River Literary Review*.

Library of Congress
Cataloging-in-Publication Data

Kastin, Darrell.
The conjurer and other Azorean tales /
Darrell Kastin.
    p.   cm.—(Portuguese in the
Americas series; 19)
ISBN 978-1-933227-41-2 (pbk.: alk. paper)—
ISBN 978-1-933227-42-9 (ebook)
1. Azores—Fiction. 2. Magic realism
(Literature) I. Title.
PS3611.A787C66 2012
813'.6—dc23   2012016945

5 4 3 2 1

FOR ELISABETH

CONTENTS

The Conjurer 1

The Last Troubadour of Lusitania 11

Dona Leonor's Dress 15

Alfredo's Timeless Death 20

Maria Almeida's Miraculous Fate 29

The Witches and the Fisherman 37

The Thief of Santa Inês 43

The Newest Star 51

The Secret Place 61

The Blind Man of Praia Negra 70

A Night on the Town 79

The Wounds 87

The Lost Voice 93

Constança's War with the Elements 99

The Exile 112

Eduardo's Promise 123

The Saint of Quebrado do Caminho 131

Night Magic 141

THE CONJURER
AND OTHER
AZOREAN TALES

The Conjurer

"NOTHING IS IMPOSSIBLE," VALDEMAR COUTINHO EXPLAINED TO HIS grandson. "With hope, an open mind, and imagination, we can find a way to recapture some of the life that has passed by, forgotten shards of memory, lost dreams."

Jorge listened to his grandfather's words, intrigued by the fierce determination that led the old man in his ceaseless attempts to unlock the mysteries the universe held in its secret heart.

"But how will we make it happen?" Jorge asked.

"By leaping into the unknown, by risking everything." His voice rose in pitch and volume.

Jorge shuddered. "And will we see beyond the stars?" he said.

Valdemar smiled. "Perhaps. Unknown and undreamt things await only the illumination of discovery, which together, you and I must find."

Jorge nodded, anxious to see the miracles of which Valdemar spoke.

People made fun of Valdemar's wild talk: "His mind is gone, poor man," Jorge heard their neighbor, Maria Fagundes, say, shaking her head with its garish plume of hair that had been dyed far too many times. "He talks of stars and light, and dreams, as if they are more important than the food one has to put on one's plate."

Maria's friend, Celia Nunes agreed. "Too many years of sitting alone on a rock in the middle of the ocean has affected him."

But Valdemar brushed off what others said about him. "Let them talk. What do I care if they laugh at me?"

Jorge's parents had brought Valdemar from the Azores, three years earlier, to live with them in their home in Gloucester, Massachusetts.

"We can't leave him on the islands," Jorge's mother had said. "He's not in any condition to take care of himself. An old man all alone—who knows what might happen to him?"

Valdemar had come reluctantly, for although he missed his family, he had one wish, and that was to be buried on the islands, which, after all, were the only home he had ever known. He had worked as a schoolteacher for many years but had retired and pursued his interest in science.

"They've uprooted me," Valdemar frequently said. "Pulled me from the soil of my past, where all my dreams and hopes were sown."

Jorge's parents both worked long hours at the small grocery store they owned, while Valdemar was left at home. They tried their best to ignore his fanciful talk, although when he spoke of such strange, unexpected things—"the melancholy song of beauty, the precipitous flights of love, the transformations of a visionary heart"—they too shook their heads and worried about Valdemar's state of mind.

"What should we do?" Jorge's mother would say. "He can't go on like this. He's an old man, why is he suddenly talking about love, about beauty?"

"Leave him be," Jorge's father would say. "When he was young he wrote poetry. Now that he's old sometimes his mind wanders and returns to those times. He's just confused."

"But what if he does something?" she said. "What if something happens?"

"What could possibly happen?" Jorge's father said. "If the old man wants to look through telescopes and pieces of glass, well then, what's the harm? It's enough that his hobby keeps him happy and out of the way."

"What about Jorge?" she said.

"Jorge can help keep an eye on him," he said. "Don't worry, they'll be fine."

In the upstairs room a variety of lenses hung from the ceiling in front of each window, and mirrors were placed at various angles to reflect each image. Valdemar's carefully arranged crystals and prisms sent out brilliant streams of light in all directions, which were captured by more lenses, and more mirrors, creating an effect of numerous rainbows and reflections, blended or superimposed one atop the other. Nothing was fixed but was always being calibrated, adjusted, fine-tuned, as Valdemar worked ever closer toward perfection.

He devised fantastic manifestations that Jorge, in his naïveté, thought were mere tricks Valdemar assembled for no other purpose than his own amusement. Jorge didn't know—until it was too late—that these so-called tricks were all part of his grandfather's serious work, which he allowed Jorge the privilege of observing—something he did for no one else.

Valdemar carefully mixed items in a beaker—a drop of sunlight, a moon-soaked bit of a dragonfly's wing, a baby's tear—heating things up, rarefying, distilling. Sometimes Jorge's parents would take Valdemar and Jorge to the Ipswich River or Chebacco Lake, on the weekend, and Valdemar would nearly always bring home a glass jar of some mysterious find that he said would help him in his pursuits.

"How do you know what we need?" Jorge asked. "And where everything is supposed to go?"

"The right things find me," his grandfather said, "allowing me to discover them when the moment is right. I merely make arrangements according to plans I see when everything else is swept from my mind."

"What do you mean?"

"It takes many years for memories to return from the beginning of time," Valdemar said, "where there is the blueprint for the future, for all that is to come."

One day Jorge entered the realm of the workshop. Instinctively, he gasped and held his breath, as his arms rose and flailed wildly. Valdemar laughed as Jorge struggled to swim. All around him the sea flowed and swirled on each of the walls. Not a print or a painting, but the living sea of swells and whitecaps bursting into foam as they broke upon the rocks.

It was as if the ocean had somehow flooded the room. Jorge spun round and round while the waves crashed. He thought his senses were deceiving him, for not only could he see the ocean but he could also hear the roar of the surf, and smell the sea breeze, while Valdemar stood gazing in pride at his handiwork.

Two days later Jorge entered the room to find the island of Pico in all its immensity: its towering volcano rose majestically inside the room.

"Look, Jorge, the island I left behind."

Jorge watched a tiny plume of smoke rise from the mountain's peak, and clouds float in and out of the room like ghostly visitors Valdemar had summoned from some other world.

Of course, Jorge wanted to know how his grandfather did these things. Not only how he made three-dimensional figures appear out of nowhere but made them so that they moved and came and went, as if they were real.

"In time," Valdemar would say, or, "It's too soon, Jorge. Have patience. Understanding will come when you are ready."

Jorge was particularly happy when Valdemar asked him to help out, to move a prism, or adjust a piece of tubing, a beaker of water, or some other object.

Jorge held a sheet of black cardboard in his hand, as Valdemar adjusted a beam of light.

"Why are there holes in the cardboard, Grandpa?" Jorge asked.

"Take one more half step to the right, Jorge," Valdemar said. "The holes are there to trick the light, to test how the light will bend."

"Light can do that?"

"A beam of light can pass through such transformations to become a droplet of the sea, and then again become something solid, like you or me. We've traveled here from the farthest reaches of the universe, Jorge. I seek to find and capture this lost light. Who knows if some night when you are asleep you will not return to your former state and become a radiant light once again?"

Jorge repeatedly dreamt of this transformation: He saw himself streaming through space like a streak of golden light. While his grandfather spoke of the sunlight that kissed the flowers, urged them to grow, and magically warmed the ocean, evaporated water, and helped create the atmosphere, Jorge imagined himself as a beam of light kissing Julia da Costa, who lived down the street, warming her cheek with the radiance with which he shone.

Sometimes Valdemar frightened Jorge, as when he entered the room to discover his grandfather standing absolutely still. *Is he dead?* Jorge wondered. Valdemar didn't respond or move for many long, torturous moments, turned to stone by concentration and perseverance, until his eyes finally reflected the image of his grandson standing there, looking worried and confused, and he winked and smiled at Jorge, his old self once again.

Another time Jorge entered to find Valdemar playing one continuous note on his viola, bowing steadily and smoothly, the note droning, as if it were liquid pouring from a fresh spring.

Valdemar sometimes trembled and spoke with an excitement that affected Jorge, too, giving them both the feeling they were on the verge of discovery.

"A wave of sound, Jorge, light and sound together, see?"

"Yes, Grandpa," Jorge said, though he wasn't sure what Valdemar was talking about. What did light have to do with sound?

"Music is a special element," Valdemar said. "There are sounds you can feel before you can actually hear them. Perhaps a bridge suspended between waves of light and waves of sound. It's in the angle of approach, the way you can see a star sometimes out of the corner of your eye, but not when you look straight at it."

Jorge wrestled with what his grandfather said, trying to conjure an image, to absorb his words in a way that would lead to comprehension.

"Certain objects," Valdemar continued, "are impossible to see from any but one angle, as when you are in a boat in the trough of a wave, you often can't see what lies beyond the crest. There are things visible only under a particular shade of light, or a certain hue. A thing can be obscured by its own radiance, or the aura of some other nearer, brighter object, and when one factors in the variable of distance, then suddenly the visible can become invisible or vice versa."

Jorge gazed up at him, uncomprehending. Maybe his grandfather really was crazy! Valdemar grabbed Jorge by the shoulder and squeezed. "Don't you see, boy, the point where waves of sound and light converge with time, which itself is a wave, each overlapping, and where together, well, who knows what we may find, eh?"

The next day Jorge came home to find Valdemar upstairs laughing with Jorge's grandmother, Maria Aurora, who had died soon after Jorge was born. Her photograph hung upon the wall, beside his grandfather's bed, and Jorge recognized her at once.

He was neither surprised nor afraid.

Jorge wondered if she would speak, but apparently she either couldn't or felt no need to; for Maria Aurora and Valdemar sat for several hours together, sharing their own past without the use of words.

After that, his grandmother began to visit regularly, always gazing at Jorge in a way that felt close, like the comforting patter of rain, or the muffled roar of the surf, and yet at the same time remote—a separateness traversed by the glow of affection and love that had come across vast distances to reach him.

Life went its usual course downstairs: minor crises concerning the grocery store arose and were resolved; visitors came and went amid the constant bustle of family life. Through it all Valdemar spent most of his time upstairs, conceiving ever more complex designs, in a maze of glass, screens, and tubes. When he did leave the house, it was only to find a book or a mirror, a lens, a clamp, or other odds and ends with which he conducted his desperate search.

Jorge would walk beside his grandfather down to the hardware store or the post office. The boys Jorge knew from school played games with other boys their own age. But Jorge sensed his own difference, his separateness from the other boys. He was drawn to his grandfather, who referred to himself as a man shipwrecked in a strange land.

"You and me, we're castaways, eh Jorge?" Valdemar would say.

Jorge would laugh and play along with the game. "Yes, Grandpa."

Valdemar would proudly state that he was a man from another time, someone born in the wrong century, pointing out that the modern world, the ordinary, run-of-the mill world, was something alien and strange to him.

"I'm like a bird on the moon," he'd say. "I have wings, but I lack the proper atmosphere for draft and lift; I cannot fly."

He lived for another time, another place. "People no longer believe in magic," he said. "They've forgotten to see the simple things for the miracles that they are; instead, they look for machines to do everything for them, forgetting that the magic is all around them and inside them as well."

Valdemar was a man made for candlelight and mysteries, with an innate, unfailing awe for the universe around him: the miracle of a sunset, a bird's flight, the sound of a baby's laughter, the wonder of water, his excitement for life, in all its munificence. Jorge didn't know anyone else who could sit and stare, completely enthralled by a puddle of water, the way his grandfather often did.

They went fishing and Valdemar would sit watching the waves unfurl, as if each were a word, a whisper, a tantalizing secret that had traversed the globe, seeking to deliver their message to his ears.

They cast their lines into the water, and while Jorge watched his line disappear into the water, Valdemar peered at the horizon, pointing, "There, Jorge, across all this ocean is home, the islands I left behind, and yet, have never left."

He told Jorge about the legends of Atlantis. "The nine islands," he said, "are the tips of great mountains, all that remain of that lost continent. Sometimes there are terrific eruptions in the ocean—fire, steam, boiling seawater, and molten rock, which cools and becomes part of the islands. Perhaps, eventually, Atlantis will rise again."

Jorge watched his grandfather but unlike the rest of the family, who saw only an eccentric old man, Jorge saw the past, alive and present; Valdemar's luxuriant green islands, surrounded by the blue sea; and the fires of hope and love in his sparkling eyes, which never seemed dull or lifeless like those of so many of the old people Jorge saw.

"We two are explorers, Jorge," Valdemar would say. "Like Pedro de Barcelos and João Fernandes Lavrador, and the others who left the Azores to search for Antília or The Island of Seven Cities. We too are searching for what others no longer believe in."

"I wish we could go to the Azores together, Grandpa," Jorge said. His parents, he knew, had no desire to return. They never spoke of the islands, as if they'd forgotten their past. Jorge had never been there. All he knew of the Azores was from what Valdemar told him.

Valdemar continued his experiments. He became excited when he read an article about newly discovered gravity waves.

"Yes, you see, Jorge, even gravity operates with waves," he exclaimed, reading from an article he'd found. "The whole universe is a sea of waves and currents, rippling, folding, unfolding." Jorge nodded, not that he fully understood, but Valdemar's enthusiasm and excitement were contagious. "The sea of humanity, too, perhaps, unconsciously operates on the principles of a living wave moving through time and space."

Valdemar had Jorge read to him from books about black holes and parallel universes. He also kept up with the latest experiments and discoveries in physics and astronomy, by having friends in Portugal mail him magazine articles. Yet he preferred to explore with his own hands, examining all the facets of a single grain of sand, as if it were the most exquisite jewel, subjecting it to every type of inquiry imaginable. And, after fitting a tiny diamond chip into the eye of a needle, used to sew sails, and focusing a beam of light on it, he said: "Imagine passing through this glass eye of a needle yourself. Where do you suppose you would end up?"

Jorge shook his head. "I don't know."

"*That* is what we will discover, Jorge," Valdemar said. "The two principal forces in the universe, Jorge, energy and inertia, life and death—which is the stronger? The force of attraction? The universe may be expanding outward, but perhaps only to reach a point where once again everything converges and becomes one again, like an inverted funnel, the lip spreading out, then folding back on itself, where the past will meet the future.

"Using the science of captured starlight, which has traveled through the vast ether of space, bringing with it the rarefied air of heaven through which it has passed, I will summon the beauteous apparition of the eyes of the lovely Maria de Conceição de Freitas, reflected in a pool of crystal water."

Several days later, Jorge came home and discovered his grandfather dancing with none other than Maria da Conceição de Freitas, a woman who had died some sixty years earlier, and Valdemar's sweetheart from the days of his youth, long before he and Jorge's grandmother had met.

Valdemar turned to Jorge as they danced, and winked. He moved like a man half his age.

∼∼∼

How his grandfather managed to disappear through the glass eye in the needle, Jorge couldn't explain. Yet, he had no doubt that was what Valdemar had done.

It was June 10, the Day of Portugal and Jorge's thirteenth birthday.

They'd had a small party downstairs. Jorge's parents bought him a new bicycle, but it was Valdemar's gifts that interested him the most: an origami book with fine-colored papers, a book on performing magic tricks—"It will do you good to learn sleight-of-hand," Valdemar said—and Valdemar's viola. "I want you to have this, to learn to play. Music expands forever, so what you play now will ring from one end of the planet to the other."

There was still one more gift to open. Jorge's parents protested. "Haven't you given him enough," Jorge's father said.

Valdemar shook his head. "Go on, open it," he said.

Jorge unwrapped the long box, and opening it, saw the telescope. There was a folded tripod, too.

"That must have cost a fortune," Jorge's mother said.

"He will need it," Valdemar said.

Jorge didn't understand, but was thrilled with the telescope.

"I can't wait to look through it," he said, rushing over to give his grandfather a hug.

"First, why don't you make me something with your origami paper?" Valdemar said.

He watched Jorge expertly fold the bright golden paper into the shape of a three-dimensional star. It was easy for Jorge, who had already gone through several books on the subject and made numerous animals and geometric shapes.

As Jorge finished making the star, however, Valdemar suddenly leaped to his feet. "Of course, folding, that's it," he muttered, "How could I have forgotten?" He quickly made his way up the stairs.

Later, Valdemar helped Jorge set up the telescope. The two of them peered at the seas of the moon. "*Maria* they are called in Latin. *Mare* is just one," Valdemar explained.

Before going to bed, Jorge entered the workroom. His grandfather was adjusting several lenses and tubes in front of the glass eye of the needle.

"Remember everything I've told you," Valdemar said. "In the end, after all my searching, it was you who gave me the answer."

"What did I do?" Jorge said.

"Your origami star," Valdemar said. "It gave me the idea of folding space and light. That was what I needed to know."

When Valdemar stepped into the center of the room, something happened. Jorge watched in amazement. He could see through his grandfather. Jorge stepped forward. Valdemar's hand rose, palm out as if to stop him. He mouthed the word "good-bye," and then appeared to slip into the beam of light focused on the tiny chip of diamond embedded in the needle's eye.

He was gone. Jorge ran to the needle. He grasped the magnifying lens, and studied the glass. He thought he saw a tiny movement, but then there was nothing, only the light.

At first, Jorge was happy, thrilled that Valdemar had finally accomplished the difficult feat which had eluded him for so long. He knew that Valdemar had planned everything out. After all, Valdemar had spoken of projections, reflections, and space-time jumps for so many years that Jorge thought nothing of it, as if Valdemar were merely talking about taking a stroll down to the park. By the next morning, however, Jorge realized that Valdemar was gone for good, and he wouldn't be coming back.

Valdemar's family phoned the police. A frantic search was made. News reports described him as helpless and sickly—neither of which was true. They made him out to be a tottering, frail man who had wandered off and forgotten where he was, who he was.

People sent flyers with his picture in a thousand directions, and television reports requested anyone who saw him to call the 800 number listed. Jorge knew it was useless, they wouldn't find him. The police investigation turned up nothing. No trace of him was found. Of course, no one cared to listen to Jorge when he tried to explain where Valdemar had gone. As far as they were concerned, he was simply a missing person, whereabouts unknown.

After several months they gave up. The family assumed he had slipped into the sea and washed away. They could imagine no other possibility for how a full-grown man could disappear. But Jorge could.

His grandfather was where he wanted to be. Valdemar had succeeded in projecting himself into the very place he sought. And who could say that by so doing he hadn't slightly, perhaps imperceptibly, altered *our* world—in essence opening the doorway a chink, creating a pathway through which others might conceivably follow?

Jorge continued to arrange the lenses, attempting to make a projection in the same way that Valdemar had used them to summon Jorge's grandmother whenever he wished to speak with her.

Sometimes, as he peered through the telescope, Jorge would see what he thought was a glimpse, a passing wisp, streaking across the night sky like a shooting star. Or he'd find a nebulous light, flaring or pulsing as if winking, communicating to some other region or far-off being, where there had only been dark, empty space before. He waved wildly, sure that Valdemar was able to see him.

Jorge hoped that, given enough time and patience, he might eventually find his way there, too; where, in another time and place, the elements would reform and perhaps the light grandfather had become would form into matter once again—a new star illuminating a distant, silent corner of space. And perhaps by then Jorge would be transformed as well: a newly formed comet or planet revolving around a bright new star.

Valdemar had found what he had been looking for, what he strove for so long to find: a way to that special realm, that place in space and time where he belonged, where there are no limits or restrictions, where past and future converged, just as he had said.

The old conjurer, even now, was probably recapturing lost moments, perhaps reciting a poem in the arms of Jorge's grandmother, if not with his beloved, Maria da Conceição de Freitas. For in Valdemar's universe there was room and love enough for both.

The Last Troubadour of Lusitania

THERE IS A LEGEND, NOW LOST TO THE EXTREME VICISSITUDES OF TIME, that long ago in the area between the Azores and the continent of Portugal lay the most fertile and beautiful of lands. This was long before Portugal was yet a country, when the Lusitanians, a mysterious Celtic tribe, then inhabited the region.

Some say an enormous island lay just offshore, Atlantis, if you will. Others insist that the mainland itself extended to the Azores, and that the islands are the last remains of that fair land, Lusitania. And in the midst of this paradise lived Pedro, the troubadour, who composed songs and sang like no other.

Pedro had always been a large man. He was known to have a strong appetite for those things which were his particular passions: food, drink, conversation, songs and stories, natural beauty, women, laughter, and living life to its fullest. When he loved there was no stopping him—no limits, and certainly no half measures. And what he loved perhaps more than anything was the countryside, the land where he was born.

From his early youth, the mountains and fields surrounding his home fascinated him. He was often seen wandering the hills and forests, the rocky outcroppings, the streams and creeks. He would seek out the oldest men and women and listen to their stories about the past, the people and the places. They told him tales about the ancient families, the history, the myths and legends of the land. And through it all, Pedro listened enraptured, drinking in every word. Then he would go wandering, singing songs, his poems—songs about this river, that hill, a valley over there, a mountain farther to the east, a beautiful girl who lived in a particular forest, or an ancient king or warrior, as if he had been taught those songs by the very places themselves.

Sometimes he would be found standing beside a tree or sitting on a rock, looking out over the view, staring so intently he wouldn't hear anyone as they approached, even if they called his name. People said he was far away, lost in the past, that he would never become a wealthy man chasing after all his dreams of inconsequential things, things that even then were beginning to fade from memory.

It was said that he knew every corner of the land, every rock and cave, every trail, the peak of every hill, as well as every ravine or gully. He knew the animals, the birds, and the properties of the plants that grew there. He knew of every hero and every villain who had passed through those parts. He knew the names of places no one else knew, old names no longer used.

And as all this took place, he grew larger, with each mouthful of sweet chestnuts, grown from the soil he roamed, with every olive produced from this land that was so special, so unique to him; for he could taste the land in everything he ate or drank: every peach, plum, or pear ripened from the sunlight, the water, and the soil.

He tried to show other people. "Here, see this spot, yes, right there, between these two hills, hear the wind that blows unlike any other? Hear that sound? The sound of the wind and the land, our land, our past." But the others shook their heads. They could not see. They did not hear. They wanted that piece of land over there in order to cut the trees, or they desired a woman from a neighboring village; they wanted wealth, or children, or a larger house, or a new boat.

But they heard Pedro sing and could feel the ebb and flow, the longing, the love and sadness conveyed in ways which made the women sigh and the men stop what they were doing and try to remember something they had forgotten long ago.

Pedro was able to recount a story for everything, always ready to sing a song or recite a poem, to quote an old saying, a proverb, even a rhyme or riddle, as well as perform the dances and the music that were part of their history.

Springs of cool, fresh water bubbled from the ground in holy, sacred places, full of spirits and magic from a time long forgotten in the past. Ghosts of the Jews of antiquity, who had sailed over from the Holy Land, of the ancient Phoenicians, the Celts who had sailed from the north, the Visigoths, then the Romans and, of course, the Moors, the Suevi, and the Gypsies as well. Each of these peoples left their mark, a trace of having lived there, in their words, in their instruments, their food and children, their music—but it was of and for the Lusitanians that Pedro lived, breathed, and sang his songs, calling to the ancient race.

Pedro drank dark red wine made from the grapes that grew here, bottle after precious bottle, as if it were sweet life itself. He drank and grew larger still.

He ate the potatoes as if they were small clumps fashioned from the very soil in which they grew, seedlings of the earth he could taste with each bite. With each mouthful he drew into himself the spirits, the music and magic of the land. Occasionally he ate an olive whole, pit and all. Sometimes, as he had done when he was a child, he ate a small piece of dirt, or a tiny stone or two. And in each taste he found a sound, a word, a meaning.

People remarked, of course, on his size. A large man, very large, teeth like the blades of a hoe, huge hands and feet. But one who could laugh and joke and tell stories like no one else.

He would sing and dance, like King Dom Pedro of old, who with whip in hand would dance through the streets of Lisbon accompanied by his band of musicians, singing and laughing, drinking, to forget his woes.

Pedro, the wandering troubadour, ate and drank, and ate and drank, and it is said that some people saw their lands shrinking or drying up, even as he grew larger.

No one, of course, dared speak the unspeakable, the impossible, that Pedro was somehow eating their lands, but they dreamed it nonetheless, and they thought it during their waking moments when they tried to work what land was left them. And they saw it, too, when they looked at the man who seemed to encompass so many fields and mounds of soil and trees, so much of his country, in his ever-increasing size, so many ancient secrets which sparkled in his eyes. But then, perhaps it was only that Pedro remembered what they had all forgotten.

Some said that when he sang they heard the breezes that once blew through the stalks of *milho painço*—millet corn—on their lands, heard the whisperings of the streams, now dried, in his voice. When thunder was heard roaring in the heavens, they said Pedro was laughing. Some claimed he baked his loaves of bread first with small amounts of soil mixed in with the fine flour produced from the neighboring fields, then used more and more soil, until finally they were nothing more than clumps of baked earth that he consumed regularly, with an unfailing appetite.

Nobody blamed Pedro for what was happening, and in fact many pointed out that, if he grew more enormous as the lands disappeared, it wasn't his fault. One or two poetic souls insisted that this was what came of forgetting; that if Pedro was so large it was because he had taken all the stories, the songs and poems, the language, the history and the myths, leaving a land stripped bare, because the people had long turned their backs on the richness of their past.

The springs continued to dry up, fields blew away, and people moved away from the villages, left the land, or simply moved farther inland to other places, found new homes and new fields to sow.

The hills and rocks, places where forests had grown, receded. Now the sea came in to fill the empty places newly made.

Pedro became a legend, a story many of the young people didn't believe, as he continued to roam, digging up the stray snippet of song, a song of a lost place, a myth of ancient seafarers and warriors.

The last few people began to leave. Not only did the land no longer hold anything for them, the land was no longer there.

For a time a large hole, like a giant rift hewn out of the earth, stood where the villages and much of the land had been. People said that Pedro was down at the bottom of that hole, for no one had seen him for some time. Sounds, it was claimed, could be heard coming from this hole, though no one cared to venture close enough to find out.

If a particularly beautiful young woman was discovered to have disappeared, she was said to be Pedro's bride, gone to join him, down at the bottom of that deepest of holes, where so much of their beloved lands had disappeared. These stories were much like the old tales of Moorish princesses who fell in love with a Christian prince or nobleman, or similar stories of Christian princesses who had fallen in love with a Moorish prince—tragic heroines who so often accompanied their lovers in death, as opposed to parting forever.

Pedro chewed the very last stones that remained, tasted the deeply buried secrets of time, his love for people and places which lay embedded in everything that filled that land, everything whose essence he had now consumed, until the waves flooded the entire region, leaving nothing but a last outcropping of rock jutting from the sea, which for generations would prove hazardous to vessels sailing along that part of the coast. And far off in the ocean, the Azores were all that remained of the western edge of the land that Pedro had consumed.

Dona Leonor's Dress

DONA LEONOR'S IRREPRESSIBLE DRESS SWEPT DOWN THE AVENIDA Diogo de Teive as if caught by a sudden covetous wind. Marveling at the playfulness of the dress, the way it fluttered and rippled ceaselessly, I followed, determined not to let it out of my sight.

I tried to drink in its colors, though none were pure or remained fixed. Instead, they changed and shifted continuously, as if liquid. It was as if each strand sought to combine with others and become not just another shade, but many different colors. There was also a language that the dress conveyed—not of words, but of something similar to the correspondences of the wind, the ocean, the flights of birds—while my heart, fanned by this language of articulate gestures, grew delirious, and urged me to gallop in mad pursuit.

I blinked and rubbed my eyes. Would this mirage suddenly vanish? Was the miracle ethereal like a rainbow, ever moving out of reach as you approached it? For miracle it was. The dress made Dona Leonor even more irresistible, and I wondered, had she made the dress more than it had been to begin with, imbuing each thread with the charm of her lively spirit, her essence?

I followed the dress past the cathedral and the cafés, then through the Praça do Infante by the waterfront. Whether Dona Leonor knew I was there, I can't say. But I would have happily pursued her over sheer cliffs, the widest deserts, or burning coals in order to keep that dress in my sight.

I had been forced to accept the harsh reality that Leonor, the beautiful youngest daughter of the noble Meneses family, could never have anything to do with me, the grandson of a poor dairy farmer, and the son of an even poorer poet. My father, self-taught and rejected by his own father, wrote a series of sonnets, as well as a book of aphorisms which summed up his personal philosophy of an intense metaphysical nature, in which the Azores and its people featured predominantly.

He taught me how to appreciate beauty in all its subtle guises, that only the grandest of dreams were worth dreaming, and that love and dreams were one and the same: "Without one you cannot have the other," he proclaimed.

We lived in the poorest section of town. Sometimes my father, pointing to a dirty, ragged-looking boy with no shoes and threadbare clothes, would say, "That child there might well be our messiah. Treat him as you would a prince."

Nobody ever took my father seriously, and it was only through my sainted mother's brother, Gil Vicente Monteiro, that I managed to get a job as a clerk in the government financial office. All my father left me when he gave up the ghost were his words, and a small collection of books.

Of course many things had changed over the years, and though Dona Leonor's aristocratic family was no longer as wealthy or powerful as it had once been, still her family and mine were separated by an unbreachable gulf. But her dress, I noted, made no such distinctions; her dress overlooked my lowly position, my humble background, my poverty.

Leonor paused on the sidewalk to chatter with some acquaintances. When she stepped into the doorway of a shop a moment later, I watched her dress slip tentatively around the edge of the entranceway, as if to see I was still there. Just the sight of its undulations made my heart ring with joy and kept my feet from resting firmly on the ground. The dress swayed and swirled around her legs, which it only partially concealed, exposing the pale flesh just above the knees, as if blown hither by the wind—yet, curiously, no breeze blew just then; the sky held its breath, unwilling to disturb the miraculous dance performed on the sidewalk below.

When Leonor entered a nearby store, I waited, leaning against the building, anxious for her to come out again, to see those patterns that left my impoverished eyes only wanting more. It reappeared suddenly like a fresh October squall. I stood frozen, unable to breathe or think or move, but the dress, with an exaggerated gesture, boldly brushed against my leg as it swept past me.

I stumbled and nearly fell, trying to regain my balance, to follow. The rest of the city, all the shops, the people milling around, the main street—everything—faded into nothingness; they were no longer real, but like ghosts to me; only Leonor's dress and myself were real.

The rest of the afternoon I was a drunken fool, a jealous lover, who trailed after the object of his desires. I followed the dress everywhere, absorbed by its quixotic life: the way it clung to her flesh, tightly, expressing every curve, and then proudly rose and flowed like newly freed waters bursting forth from some remote chasm.

The dress disappeared into the doorway of a building and minutes passed before I realized that it wouldn't be coming out again anytime soon. We had come to Leonor's home.

I stood lost, unable to move, staring at the building. So close, yet still so far beyond my reach. Though no longer visible, the lingering memory of movements, now languid and smooth, then wildly paced and strikingly bold, entranced me.

I stood waiting on the street. Soon her bedroom window was lit upstairs. I watched as the dress was hung up. One sleeve motioned toward me, a gesture to show it was pleased I was still there yet obviously saddened at the terrible distance which now stretched between us.

The house grew quiet as everyone settled in for the night. The dress hung, perhaps motionless, in the stillness of the enclosed space. Or did it tremble restlessly, unable to sleep?

I fought against the urge to climb to the window, wanting nothing so much as to touch that material, to hold it in my hands for a moment and let it whisper its secret rustlings in my ear.

I stood vigil the entire night, fixed like a stone statue, buffeted by the elements. I was unaware of the cold, or hunger, or loneliness, for I was warmed by the visions I possessed of Dona Leonor's dress. I dreamt of the two of us wandering together, how it would perhaps strive to be more than a mere dress, as was already so apparent in its nature.

I envisioned the two of us shipwrecked, afloat on some planks of timber, wherein the dress, in order to save me, formed itself into a taut sail. I saw us sleeping in fields while it curled around me, protectively serving as a blanket, warming me in the damp night. I smiled at the thought of strumming a *guitarra*, or playing a violin, and watching the dress dance, a vision of beauty, imparting meaning with each subtle movement in that sublime language that connected the two of us to our very core.

I prayed the dress would fly off its hanger and float down to where I stood. Perhaps it tried but couldn't remove itself from the fixture. I heard it whisper to me, the maddening rustle of soft cloth.

In the morning I was still there, stiff and half-asleep, my whole body aching. But when I saw the flash of that bright dress spring forth from the front door, like hope itself, once again my spirits soared. I forgot about my aching muscles, my sore back, forgot everything but that dress, which fluttered, as if it could barely restrain itself; it was so alive, in spite of the two hands that in a futile gesture kept reaching to keep it down.

I followed it to a room in the office building where Dona Leonor worked. I decided to go home and clean myself up, though it was nearly impossible to tear myself away. As I walked I noticed the many dresses I passed and was surprised to realize how different they were; they hung drab and lifeless, their colors monotonous, without any spark. There was no vibrancy compared to *her* dress.

The entire day I dreamt of the dress, moved by the sound of a mere flutter, lightheaded and breathless as I imagined my hand touching it, or smelling its fresh scent, kissing every stitch along its marvelous hem.

That evening I made my move, entirely unplanned yet unavoidable. My father's words, "Beauty makes its own cause," came to mind.

I went to her house and peered over the fence into the yard. There was a clothesline that ran alongside the building. And to my amazement, hanging from the clothesline, I found the dress, waving wildly, trying desperately to get my attention.

Without thinking, I unlatched the fence and stepped into the yard. I instantly unhooked the dress. My hands shook as it fell into my arms, spent and relieved I assumed, from its hours of demonstrations, or perhaps the uncertainty of wondering whether I would show up.

I folded the dress carefully and left the yard before anyone observed me. I quickly made my way down the street without so much as a glance backward. If someone had shouted or come after me I knew I would have had to flee. But as it was, no one saw and no one followed. The dress and I had escaped. My body thrilled to the feel of the dress in my arms, the way it nestled against my side. It was difficult to believe we had done it! I rushed home, taking side streets the entire way.

All my secret expectations have been fulfilled. The dress is remarkable, as I knew when I first saw it. I have acquired a dressmaker's dummy—though it cost me considerable trouble—upon which it fits beautifully. It is obviously proud and happy. Its carefree flow, the way it reaches out to touch me when I stand near is both reassuring and exhilarating.

Its ever-shifting patterns and colors please and delight the eye: rows of blood-red hearts one moment, then hundreds of waves curling, spray flying from their crests, or blue and white birds suddenly taking flight.

At night, with the window flung wide open and the rising moon bathing us in its milky light, I put on some music and the two of us swim, sail, float across the floor, free of gravity and all else—just the two of us, Dona Leonor's dress and me dancing on air.

Alfredo's Timeless Death

ALFREDO BETTENCOURT SPOKE ABOUT HIS IMPENDING DEATH SO OFTEN and for so long that everyone living in the village of Quebrado do Caminho became swept up in the excitement and expectation that grew with each passing day, week, and month. After some time, people forgot exactly what he was dying of, but that only added to the impressive weight and magnitude of his death, until nothing else mattered. It was as if time had stopped and events in the village had come to a standstill, everyone holding their collective breath, awaiting the resolution of Alfredo's imminent death.

Quebrado do Caminho was situated at the bottom of a secluded rift between the towns of Santa Luzia and Santo António, on the island of Pico in the Azores. It was a forgotten place, too small to be remembered and too insignificant to be noticed by anyone who may have passed by. The village had been abandoned long ago, after a severe earthquake destroyed many of the buildings. At that time, most people simply moved farther up the mountain and built a new village, leaving the ruins of the old one behind. Some, however, wished to remain in their old familiar homes, where generation after generation of their families had lived. So these few determined souls rebuilt what they could and remained in Quebrado, cut off from all the other towns and villages. It was the kind of place one could find only by accident, but it happened so rarely that the villagers thought of themselves and Quebrado do Caminho as the entire world.

Each time Alfredo stepped into the café or the *taberna* his neighbors rushed to buy him drinks, as they would for any good friend who, in a day or two, was going off on a long journey. He couldn't pass someone's house without being called inside for a meal or a drink of *angelica* or *aguardente*. If he didn't appear for a day or two, people would come by to check with his friends and neighbors.

"Is it time?" they asked. "Has he gone?"

"No, not yet," the others answered. "He still lives."

"Thank God!"

Everyone in the village had long ago decided how they would respond when the moment finally did arrive. They knew precisely what they would do and the things they would say: Rui, the stone mason, would tell tall tales of Alfredo, the ladies' man, of his cavorting with numerous unnamed women—who didn't exist, except in Rui's imagination; João Carlos, the baker, would give a fine speech about Alfredo's honesty and biting wit, neither of which he possessed; even Pacheco, the laundress, had in mind to utter a few humorous asides, to lighten the mood, since Alfredo always loved a good joke.

The people of the village even had the funeral planned out, since Alfredo spoke often of how he would like it to be. The only problem was that Alfredo frequently changed his mind about how his funeral should be conducted.

Just when the villagers knew they were to bury him beside his mother and father in the small local cemetery, Alfredo suddenly decided that he should be buried instead on Corvo, where his grandfather had been born; then he insisted on being buried up the steep slopes of Pico, and later that he should be buried at sea.

Still, he was dying, and such caprices must be tolerated, no matter how inconvenient and bothersome they might be for the living.

One day he met his old friend, José Vicente, along the road.

"Good day, Alfredo," José said. "How are you holding up these days?"

"Not bad for a dead man."

"You're giving Old Man Death quite a chase, no?"

"It's best not to rush this sort of thing," Alfredo said.

"No, I guess not," José said. "It seems that death, too, knows the word *amanhã*."

"Yes, so it does," Alfredo said, laughing. The two men leaned against a tree and each rolled a cigarette. José offered Alfredo a light.

"But you still look pretty good," José said, examining Alfredo's appearance. "Especially given, you know, your condition."

"I'm beginning to think death suits me, José. Who knows—perhaps I can die better than I lived."

José nodded thoughtfully. "You think maybe he has forgotten about you?"

"I don't know what to think," Alfredo said. "I've had very little experience with dying."

"Well, how do you feel? Do you feel that death is very close?"

Alfredo nodded. "If I were to judge for myself, I would say that chances are I'm quite close to death. I'm old, and my bones have grown weary. Yes, I should think that any time now, perhaps tonight, death will come fetch me, and I shall go."

José Vicente crossed himself several times. "May you rest in peace, my friend."

"Thank you, José. I must go now."

"Take care, then, Alfredo. Until soon."

"If God should will it," Alfredo said. "Good day, José."

Alfredo walked away. "Why tell a dying man to take care? What does a dead man have to worry about? Catching a cold? Might I trip and break my neck?"

He chuckled to himself as he walked back to the village. He didn't see the cart loaded down with hay until it had run him over. He got up and dusted himself off.

"Ha, ha! Be careful, Alfredo. Better watch out, you might get killed. It's a joke, no?"

He looked himself over, and shouted after the cart, "Hey, did you see? I wasn't killed!"

In the early morning, Alfredo went down to the quay, as if inspecting which boat might take him on his final journey. He jumped into the water to see if he would drown, but it didn't work, no matter how long he stayed under.

"I knew it," he shouted. "Someone is trying to cheat me out of my own death."

In the middle of the night Alfredo could be seen walking through the streets or along the road out of town, heedless of carts, wagons, or horses that might have run him over, because once a man believes he is impervious to death he feels it incumbent upon himself to defy again and again that fate from which he has escaped, as if flaunting his miraculous luck.

"Is this right?" Maria Teresa asked. "Why, all of a sudden, is he carrying on so much, everywhere at once? Why isn't he at home in bed where a dying man should be?"

"Perhaps he thinks he can hide," João Roberto said. "He's trying to find a place where death hasn't yet been."

"There is no such place," Miguel Mendes declared.

"He should settle down and die already," Maria Teresa said. "And be done with it."

The children of the village were greatly impressed with Alfredo's death, which by this time had become legend, and they anxiously awaited the event. They regarded Alfredo as a hero, the likes of whom hadn't been seen for many, many years. They believed the event would transform the village—indeed, the entire island. They were sure that miracles would occur on a scale never before seen, although they never bothered to explain exactly what they thought would happen. Instead, they said, "You'll see," and watched the skies, eager to find any sign or portent of the miracles certain to come.

Even when their parents began dying off, the children, who remained children, knew that it was somehow preparatory and necessary to the greater death to come.

Alfredo often found a group of the children waiting for him by the docks or in front of the market. "Mariazinha," he said, patting one child's head. "And you, Miguel, don't be afraid of anything. You listen to your uncle Alfredo. Don't let anyone tell you different." He would hand them some berries gathered on one of his walks.

One day his neighbor, Maria Isabel, found Alfredo two or three kilometers from the village. He was walking along the road in the wrong direction. She had gone to bring a meal to her husband tending their cows. She was surprised to find Alfredo out there.

He didn't see her until she shouted at him: "Alfredo! What are you doing?"

He stared at her. His face was without expression.

"Are you asleep?"

Alfredo rubbed his jaw. "No. I don't think so."

"What is wrong?"

"Nothing."

"Well, what are you doing, then?"

"Looking."

"Did you lose something?"

"See there," he said, pointing at the ground beside his feet. "I have no shadow."

"Oh, sweet sainted Mother of God, you *are* a dead man!" Maria rolled her eyes toward heaven and ran away, leaving Alfredo all alone, searching for his lost shadow. She returned to her husband, Rui Gomes, and told him what she had seen. The two of them rushed back to the village as quickly as they could and told everyone how Maria Isabel had seen Alfredo, who no longer cast any shadow.

Later that same day, the children of the village were seen following Alfredo.

"What next?" cried Maria Teresa. "Hasn't this gone on long enough? Someone should put a stop to this foolishness once and for all!"

"Careful, woman. You might blaspheme," Miguel Mendes said, raising his eyes toward heaven.

It was generally agreed that Maria Teresa was a reckless woman. No one else in the village was about to say much concerning this thing that none of them understood, especially since it was generally agreed that the supernatural might be involved with Alfredo and the children.

He was seen leading them at all times of the day and night, along the roads in and around the village, down by the quay, or the rocks along the shore, and up the steep slopes of the mountain toward the *caldeira*, bellowing volcanic smoke.

The children came home infrequently and often spoke mysteriously about things that frightened the old people. Alfredo had taught them to talk with the animals, they said, to stay under water for days at a time, and converse with the dead.

"God help us,'" the people cried. "Only ruin can come of this!"

∾ ∾ ∾

After a number of years, many of the people who had known Alfredo had passed on, but his name had by no means been forgotten. It was on one cold windless night that his old friend José Vicente saw Alfredo walk out of the water and come toward him.

"Alfredo," José said, with a heavy sigh. "Still not dead, I see."

"Good evening, José. I'm happy to see you are alive, as well."

"Everybody is dying, old man. Myself, and a few others are all that's left. Why aren't you dead yet?"

Alfredo shrugged. "I don't know. Perhaps it's still not my time."

"Hell, we will all be dead before you are."

"Who knows what God intends for any of us. Until next time, José."

The next day José Vicente told those villagers who were still alive about his talk with Alfredo.

"I told you it was a bad thing," said Maria Teresa. "He's taken the children. What have we got left but a dead village?"

"Be still, woman," Miguel Mendes said. "It's beyond our comprehension. Some things weren't meant for us to understand."

"But who will fish and tend the cows?" João Almerindo asked.

"Or make the wine?" Manuel Vieira wanted to know.

"We should talk to Padre Silveira," Maria Isabel said.

They went to see the padre and explained the situation, of which he already knew many of the particulars. They begged him to do something.

"I'm not sure what I can do," he said, cautiously.

"Can't you declare him dead?" Maria Teresa said. "He should lie down and be quiet like all good dead people."

"But I need a body, some proof that he is deceased." The padre was clearly afraid of embroiling himself in something that he saw as beyond the scope of his experience, uncertain as to whether this had to do with God and heaven or was some sinister ploy of angry witches or some other minion of the devil. "What's more," he said. "I need to know the moment of death, or at least how long he has been dead."

This thoroughly confused everybody because no one could agree on when Alfredo had passed away. Since he had continued to live after losing his shadow and resisted death by drowning, falling, being run over several times, and numerous other instances, the padre declared that for all practical purposes, he was still a living man, as far as he could ascertain, and as such, he was in no position to be pronounced dead.

Alfredo was seen again and again, looking older but no less alive. He shouted unintelligible words at the clouds, sun, and moon; even the waves behaved strangely in his presence. The villagers often heard him speaking to the goats and cows, and sometimes, those aboard the fishing boats observed him swimming with the whales and dolphins. Except for the children, he hardly spoke at all to any of the remaining townspeople and, in fact, rarely seemed to notice them. No one understood anything he said anymore.

"He is *louco*, at last," people said to one another, nodding.

Still the children, who remained children no matter what the old and dying said or did, produced the offerings of miracles they had long ago prophesied.

Little Emanuel paraded a hermaphrodite goat; Maria Luisa da Costa e Silva carried about her two-headed chicken; three of the children were deaf and dumb and so given the stature of minor divinities; Eriana "Ninha" Pacheco carried her baby within her virgin womb for eighteen months before delivering the child at night under the waves, tearfully watching it swim off for the open sea, its fin slipping effortlessly through the water, moonlight glistening off its scales.

Alfredo spent more and more of his time at the top of the mountain.

The padre continued his Sunday Mass and didn't appear to notice that the only people who attended his services were ghosts.

Seasons changed and brought bright fruits and vegetables of enormous size in winter and in the fall, and flowers that bloomed every other month. *Maracujá* and oranges grew the size of melons, *nêsperas* the size of pears, and fresh water suddenly began flowing from a spring in the ground. The children waded into the ocean and caught fish which leaped into their hands.

Delightfully warm rains fell and, on occasion, the sun stayed in the sky for several days. The children gathered one night and watched as the moon settled on the mountain, brought there, of course, by Alfredo, who was still up to his old tricks.

The children played, and made up poems and songs about their village and about the legend of the great timeless death of Alfredo. They continued to gather the special animals born with three legs or two heads, and lived without any regard for the outside world, perhaps without even knowing that they were not following the ways of their parents and grandparents.

Finally, Alfredo's friend, José Vicente, now extremely old and one of the few remaining villagers alive, decided to take matters into his own hands.

"As long as Alfredo is alive," José said. "Nothing will ever change around here."

So José Vicente went off in search of Alfredo, prepared to bring Alfredo the death that had eluded him for so long and return his village at last to normal.

"I hope he finds him," Maria Teresa said. "This should have been done a long time ago."

José Vicente swore he wouldn't come back without first delivering Alfredo to the very gates of heaven. He marched up the side of the mountain, disappointed that the children he spoke to refused to tell him whether Alfredo had swum off, or flown, or gone up to the mountaintop and climbed onto the back of the moon making its way across the sky.

∼∼∼

Many, many years later, a bent and frail old man stumbled into the village. His eyes were opaque with cataracts, his skin grew like the bark of the trees, his hair was a tangled nest of silver and gray, and his limbs resembled the spindly branches of the fava trees more than human arms and legs.

A group of people was hard at work in the village—strangers who had come on a large boat. They were cutting down huge plants and vines, many of which crisscrossed the roads and completely covered the houses. A small group of nuns and priests was busy officiating over the recitation of prayers and splashing holy water everywhere.

The old man walked until he found a yard being used to slaughter the huddled groups of deformed animals. Blood pooled in the mud and an overpowering stench filled the air.

A group of children was being led toward a boat that had come to take them away. The old man stared at the children as they passed. Some of them looked up at him, as well. His own child, Joana Maria, didn't recognize him, nor did José Vicente recognize her.

He passed the people working and opened his mouth to speak, but no one could make out a word he said. They heard gibberish, and assumed he was senile.

"Hey, you," someone shouted. "Old man!" He was gently grabbed by the arm and pulled to face one of the workers. "Are you coming with us or are you staying behind?"

The old man's lips moved without a sound.

"Who are you?"

The old man shook his head.

"Everyone in this village is dead except for some poor children, who are, you know," he said, touching the side of his head. He peered at the old man's face and spoke slowly in a loud voice. "Even the old padre was just a skeleton, kneeling in prayer in the church. It looks as if we are the first people to arrive in, hell, who knows how many years. Are you from here?"

José Vicente made a hoarse wheezing sound.

"Hey, João, hurry up," one of the other workers shouted. "There's still work to do."

"Patience. I'm coming. Good-bye, old man." He returned to the group of workers.

José Vicente turned around and shuffled down the dirt road back toward the mountains, mumbling and muttering to himself. His eyes shone, alive with the light of one who has searched the back of the moon and beyond, the look of one who has wandered a landscape where time performed strange permutations and sleights of hand, as he set out once more to follow the slippery trail of Alfredo Bettencourt's timeless and elusive death.

Maria Almeida's Miraculous Fate

THE TRUTH, OR RATHER THE ENTIRE TRUTH, IT IS SAFE TO SAY, WILL never be known—at least not with any certainty. Some say that the day Maria Leonor Almeida washed up on the sands of Quebrado do Caminho was the day the devil rose from his foul depths to plague the village. Others insist it was no less than a miracle, that God and a host of saints were involved.

"The girl is blessed," they murmured. "Someone to be admired and feared."

Old Palmira, the *benzedeira*, was summoned in order to remove the evil spell some believed had been placed on the girl. Even still, Maria Leonor's grandmother shut herself in her room and refused to eat, drink, or sleep, praying continuously, "until this shame is finally removed from our house and family."

Maria Leonor claimed to have no idea what had taken place, but anyone could see her eyes gleamed, transfixed; as if she gazed at something in the distance. Soon she was unable to speak, but uttered only strange incomprehensible noises.

The events of those mysterious few weeks are shrouded by conflicting reports and irresponsible conjecture, which—along with the conflagration of hysteria—swept over the entire village. Needless to say, nothing of this nature had ever occurred on the island of Pico or on any of the Azores, for that matter.

Maria Leonor's father, Senhor João Gilberto Almeida, the proud and wealthy owner of some of the island's finest pastures and cows, turned a deaf ear and a blind eye to the events, burying himself in his work as well as his hobbies, shooting his collection of antique firearms and working as an amateur genealogist, researching the ancient origins of his family tree, which traced its obscure beginnings to the eighth century. He simply refused to believe or even acknowledge that anything unusual was taking place. Throughout all the following events he maintained an impassive silence; there was an air of imperial fortitude in this last of the monarchists, a man who had seen so many changes transpire during his lifetime.

No one could agree on how Maria Leonor had ended up on the beach. Senhor Fraga said the girl had floated, clinging to a large piece of wood, and been carried by the waves to the shore; Dona Maria da Cunha believed Maria Leonor had flown, although she was at a loss to say how; Senhor Velas claimed he saw her walk out of the waves on her own two feet. Maria's mother would only say that an angel must have refused to allow Maria Leonor to die and had come down at that moment to save her daughter's life, protecting her from the shame of drowning.

"Only the most wretched people drown," Senhora Almeida said. "Poor people who haven't a thing, not even a name. No one with the name Almeida has ever died an improper death; we die only at a time and in a manner that God sees fit."

What *is* certain is that, one week earlier, Maria Leonor had left her home in the late afternoon and walked down to the sea. Voices, she later said, called to her again and again. Sweet voices, melodic and musical—"angelic voices," Maria Leonor insisted—called her name, whispering their muffled messages, which she had followed as she attempted to decipher their meaning.

She remembered approaching the waves without fear, curious, yet completely at peace. As to the question, Did she try and drown herself? No one could say with any certainty. She herself did not remember, except that one moment she had been standing, listening as she watched the progression of the waves, on the verge of understanding what the sounds filling her ears meant, when suddenly she was swept away, held aloft by the rising water, and carried out to sea.

Senhora Almeida loudly insisted that no one with the name Almeida would ever attempt suicide. "*We* do not sin," she said, with conviction and defiance.

Miguel Carneiro, a fisherman from Madeira, who'd come to Quebrado do Caminho after a failed and infamous romance with a married woman, had been sailing back to the harbor with a sizable catch after several days at sea. The weather was fair and the sea was calm.

He kept his eyes trained on the stretch of water that lay between him and the island, steering for the spot of land where he would soon moor his boat and come ashore. He would head for the tavern and drink his fill, hoping to forget the doleful dark eyes of Dona Rosa de Melo.

While still several kilometers away from the village, Miguel spotted a group of dolphins. He smiled, for they were the only companions he had while at sea. The dolphins swam alongside his boat and leaped playfully in the water. He heard their laughter as they appeared to glance over at him, the twinkle in their eyes seeming to say, "Hello there. Come, let's have some fun!"

Miguel waved and laughed. Then he saw that one in their midst wasn't a dolphin at all, but a woman, rising then diving into the waves, her hair made sleek by the water. Did he know her? Was he really seeing what he thought? He shook his head, shutting then reopening his eyes.

Just as suddenly as they had appeared, the dolphins, with the woman he perhaps recognized among them, swam away. He tried to steer the boat toward the dolphins, but at once the sea turned choppy; the waves slapped the boat back with sudden force, as if to prevent him from following.

Stunned and muttering to himself, in a state of complete confusion, Miguel reached the dock. He tied the boat and stumbled to the Taberna Mendes, where he remained until closing, attempting to wash down the persistent image of an enticing young woman with flawless skin, swimming through the water with a swarm of dolphins.

Maria Leonor, when she was later found, was thoroughly examined by the schoolteacher, Eduína Fagundes, because there was no doctor in the village. Even if there had been one, people would have looked upon him with suspicion, trusting in medical doctors only as a last resort, and then often only to assure a speedier route to one's grave.

"If the prognosis is in doubt," Maria Leonor's grandmother declared, "call in a doctor. He'll walk in with death at his side."

Maria Leonor was taken home, and no one saw or heard from her for many days.

"She is giving thanks," her mother said. "Since she was dragged out of the sea more dead than alive, only by the miracle and intervention of Our Lady, who, as the Mother of God, naturally felt pity and compassion and decided to spare our poor child, Maria Leonor has since felt the terrible burden of eternal gratitude and has resolved to pray, with her sainted grandmother, until her own heart has found her debt satisfactorily repaid."

Senhora Almeida found it impossible to speak without making a speech, perhaps to compensate for her husband's reticence. But the truth was that Maria Leonor hadn't fully recovered from her experience and was quite ill. This was learned from Carlota Santos, the maid of a neighbor, who was said to have heard it from one of Senhora Almeida's own servants.

"It's just as though the land has made her seasick," Carlota explained.

Maria Leonor was in a terrible state and remained shut away in her room. She was constantly attended and watched over by her mother, by her aunts and her sisters—a vigil of candles and prayers, of tears and lamentations, of threats and pleadings. Only one of the maids, Maria Estreita, who had been with the family the longest, was allowed near her. The long hours of exposure to the sea, the lack of food and fresh water, and the unexpected shock resulting from her experience had created lasting ill effects.

Neighbors attempted to visit the house, eager to learn more and see for themselves what condition the girl was in. They dressed in their best and came armed with an insatiable curiosity, but the maids were instructed not to permit any visitors into the house, which sent more than one neighbor off in a huff, gravely insulted, driven to anxiety by their desire to know all the details of what was occurring without their knowledge.

The Almeidas' maids and servants were each questioned daily on the streets or in the markets, often bribed with offerings of sweets.

"Did you hear?" whispered Dona Maria da Cunha, as she stood outside the jeweler's shop. "Maria Leonor is being kept alive with buckets of seawater."

"What?"

"I heard it just this morning. They're bringing seawater into the house and pouring it over her."

The other women murmured to themselves.

"She sits in a tub of salt water all day and night."

Senhor Fraga, after the church service, told what he had heard. "They say that she tried to jump from the upstairs window and they had to tie her up."

"But why?" someone asked.

"Because she wishes to return to the sea. They say it draws her, as if during her days in the ocean her blood had been replaced with seawater."

"Perhaps King Neptune himself has won her heart," another added.

"Ahh."

Alvaro de Palma, the old whale lookout, came forward. "I saw Maria Leonor standing on the back of an enormous whale," he said, "the likes of which I have never seen before, the greatest of all whales. I was so surprised by what I saw that I even forgot to sound the alarm announcing a whale had been spotted." But the whalers who listened to Alvaro de Palma eyed him with some doubt, thinking he was drunk again.

Of course, no one could confirm or deny the authenticity of these stories, which at times exceeded the natural limits of plausibility. However, they continued in this manner until the startling revelation, which instantly transformed even the most persistent doubters: Maria Leonor Almeida was pregnant.

The news traveled to every corner of Quebrado do Caminho like a bolt of lightning. Horror and disbelief were expressed in the streets and carried from open window to open window. How did this happen? Who was the father? Was she raped? Had she knowingly seduced one of the young men of the village?

While most of the men were more than a little surprised, many of the women were upset; for, except for the one or two braggarts who claimed to have always noticed something peculiar about the girl, the rest were at a complete loss to explain Maria Leonor Almeida's condition. After all, no one had ever really taken any notice of her. They had always thought of her as an absolutely unexceptional girl, not worthy of anyone's attention. If someone had bothered to point her out they would have all probably shaken their heads and exclaimed: "Her? Why, I had forgotten all about her!" Now, however, all that had changed. Now no one could forget her or talk of anything else.

"She was always a quiet girl," one neighbor said. "A good girl."

"Yes, but she always did have a far-off look in her eyes," said another.

"That's right, a dreamy nature."

"And always singing, too, songs no one else seemed to know," said another. "A simple child."

Suspicion fell almost immediately upon Miguel Carneiro, the fisherman. After all, people were quick to point out, he had been gone about the same amount of time as Maria Leonor. He had returned to the village and drank himself useless, talking crazy talk about dolphins and a girl who swam among them. Even now, after all this time, he still hadn't gone back out to sea. Not to mention the fact that he had a reputation for scandal, which he wore like a large and heavy chain, and of which he could never rid himself.

Miguel, however, brushed aside their suspicions. "It might have been her that passed my boat in the water with the dolphins. I don't know. But I never laid a hand on her."

Maria Leonor remained in her room, but could be seen at all hours peering from her window at the ocean. People walked past and looked up to see her staring at the waves in the distance, at the sunlight playing upon the water.

Women crossed themselves and men shook their heads. "*Coitadinha*—poor thing! Look at her. You'd think her lover had been lost at sea."

At night, Maria could be heard singing—the notes and words exotic and unknown to the ears of those who listened, although everyone who heard recognized the sounds of longing. The night air was filled with the sound of her voice and the murmurs of waves and currents, the silvery flash of fish and dolphins swimming across the channel—all the creatures to which she sang, imploring them to take her, to swim to her side.

The months passed and Maria Leonor's belly grew swollen with her mysterious child, who, it was said, swam unceasingly like a fish caught in the tiny sea within her womb.

Alicia Mendes, a woman from São Jorge or Graciosa who had assisted in a number of difficult pregnancies, was summoned by Senhora Almeida to stay by her daughter's side and assist with the birth.

Caring for the girl was not an easy task. She wept almost constantly and thrashed about when she slept. Sometimes she sat listless and sullen, watching the rolling sea from her bedroom window, as she moaned and whimpered throughout the day and night.

Alicia Mendes suggested that Maria stay in another room of the house, one that did not face the shore, for the sea, she said, upset the girl. But when they tried to move her Maria screamed, tearing at her hair and threatening to gouge out her own eyes, so they quickly gave up on the idea.

The only thing that appeared to calm her was the constant application of fresh seawater, brought up to the room by one of the children, and squeezed from a sponge over the girl's writhing body. Then Maria Leonor's breathing once more became regular, and her sobbing would grow quiet.

Finally the hour had come. Alicia Mendes worked feverishly on the girl, who now pushed away the warm towels and cried out for more water instead—neither hot water nor drinking water, but cold seawater.

"More water," Alicia said to the servants who were stationed outside the door, waiting for her orders. "Quickly!" She kept them hopping down to the shore, fetching bucketful after bucketful.

Maria Leonor appeared to be in excruciating pain but calmed down and was nearly silent, making only strange gurgling sounds and moving wildly about the bed, by then soaked with seawater and sweat.

Alicia Mendes was sure the baby would come at any moment, and she prepared everything in order to deliver the child.

She turned her back for one moment to grab a towel and—before she knew it or could do anything about it—Maria Leonor rose out of the bed, grabbed hold of the sheets, and fled through the door.

"How can she run?" Alicia said in disbelief. "And in her condition?"

The house was instantly thrown into an uproar. There were cries and shouts from the women, the silent continuous prayers of Maria Leonor's grandmother, and expressions of helplessness from the servants and men of the family. Everyone filed out of the house after Maria Leonor, except for Senhor Almeida, who proceeded to finish his midday meal in glum silence, as if nothing had happened.

Maria Leonor ran down to the water. As she passed by, activity on the streets came to a standstill—until the family rushed past, and then everyone followed to see what would happen next.

They reached the shore, but there was no sign of her. Then someone shouted. "Look, over there!" He pointed at the waves. Maria Leonor rolled about in the water. She dove suddenly and after a moment surfaced again. Several men waded into the water. Her family begged her to come out, shouting that she and the baby would drown.

Maria instead turned on her back. Her legs came up out of the water, and she gave a short, piercing cry as something silvery flashed and disappeared between her legs, sleek and agile as a fish.

There was an audible gasp from her family, friends, and neighbors who stood helplessly on the shore.

"What is it?" someone murmured.

"A fish?" said another.

"Dear Mother of God!"

Several women fainted.

"Looks like a dolphin."

"A devil."

In a moment there were others in the water—fish, dolphins, and more, all churning up the sea. Maria Leonor turned around and waved good-bye to her family, then swam with the other creatures out to sea, as the stunned villagers looked on.

In the distance, Miguel Carneiro's boat could be seen heading out to sea for the first time since he had come back talking about a girl who swam with dolphins.

The Witches and the Fisherman

IN THE SMALL FISHING VILLAGE OF POVOAÇÃO, ON THE ISLAND OF SÃO Miguel, no one had to ask who was the best fisherman. Miguel Luís Reis always brought in the largest catch and, according to Domingos Braga, who supplied most of the fishermen with drink, it was all because of the witches.

"He is charmed," Domingos Braga would tell you. "Ever since the night the witches took him away, the fish practically leap aboard his boat."

It was several years back when Miguel Luís Reis began to notice strange things about his boat.

For seven days he had left his house and walked down the stone street to the waterfront only to find his boat, not as he had left it, but moved, lying at an odd angle, even completely turned around, facing the wrong way, as if to taunt or mock him. There might be something missing, or a foot of water sloshing inside the hull; his tackle would be in a mess, and his nets tangled. But that wasn't all. Miguel often discovered things inside the boat that hadn't been there the day before: a pile of fine sand, a suspicious piece of cloth, or a snag of unfamiliar leaves—and always from plants that he had never seen growing on the island.

He crept to his boat late one night, and again the following night, but to his surprise found no sign of whoever was using him as the butt of this practical joke. What could it mean except that, in the hours after midnight and before dawn, witches were using his boat for their own purposes?

"I will not be made a fool of by witches," Miguel Luís Reis declared, stomping his foot on the beach. "I'm going to put an end to this once and for all."

Although Miguel Luís was afraid of what the witches might do if he confronted them, he also wasn't about to permit his boat to be confiscated for their nefarious uses. After all, a man has a special relationship with his boat. Sailing alone on the vast ocean day after day, a man and his boat developed a close bond. He depended on the vessel to return him safely to port, and he learned how to maneuver her with expert skill, so that the boat responded to his slightest movement.

He decided to lay a trap and catch the culprits.

He dressed warmly, wrapped in his heavy coat, and once again sneaked down to his boat late at night, carrying a bottle of *aguardente*. He lay down in the bow and covered himself with the tarp that was usually stowed there, which concealed him quite nicely. He peered out and kept watch for any sign of the witches.

It was cold and uncomfortable, but Miguel was used to it. After all, he made his living on the sea. The hours passed slowly. Miguel wished he could light a fire for warmth, but of course that was impossible. He struggled to keep his eyes open.

"I'm sure to catch the witches," he said to himself. He would surprise them when they showed up and, with luck, they would fly off, back to their lair—wherever that might be. At least he hoped they would flee. The only thing he carried for protection, other than a stick, was a branch of laurel leaves, since they were said to be best for warding off evil.

After many cold hours, the calm of night was broken by the sound of laughter—a shrill, unnatural laughter like the horrible shriek of the old-time carts one still saw at the time, the kind with wooden axles, left ungreased by their owners to annoy the world with the tortured scraping of wood against wood.

But this was worse. The terrible sound jarred Miguel awake, his eyes opened wide in fright.

The first thing he noticed was that the boat was moving. Quickly. It wasn't sailing, however. He'd spent enough time on the water to know when the boat was riding the swells and when it was not. This was not sailing. It was flying.

He gasped and peered over the prow into the dark water. The boat was soaring over the ocean, several feet above the water, and at a dizzying speed.

Three witches, pale as chalk and hideous as sin, huddled in the stern of the boat, laughing and cackling and making a grand time of it.

An old cauldron, blacker than a moonless night, sat before them, and into this they kept dropping God-only-knows-what, retrieved from the deep pockets of their clothing, which hung in tatters, a hodgepodge of dizzying grays, whites, blacks, and the nameless shades in between.

They took turns stirring their brew, uttering words that to Miguel's ears were shrieks, croaks, and curses, as the cauldron hissed and boiled each time the witches dropped something new in it.

Miguel drank from his bottle, hoping that the spirits he drank would shatter the nightmarish vision before his eyes. But the visions persisted.

Amid the cackles and shouts of the witches, Miguel determined that they had reached the Arabian sands, then India, Timor, China, and Japan—where they picked up a very black and glowering cat, as large as a small dog, with eyes that gleamed bright yellow—before the boat swung round and they came up to the Island of the Moon: Madagascar.

Miguel recognized each of these places because one of the witches—the tallest, leanest one—announced every arrival, as though she were some supernatural tour guide.

Each pronouncement was followed by yet another fit of coarse laughter.

The boat slowed momentarily, then Miguel sighted the mountains of the Horn of Africa. There the witches screeched one word over and over, like the name of a delicacy they wished to savor: *Adamastor! Adamastor! Adamastor!*

Scared and shivering as he peered from beneath the tarp, Miguel stared at the ocean below and saw a towering shape materialize in the darkness. He heard the roar of the monster whose bellows shook the world. The witches laughed, hiccupped, and burped.

Then, the boat sped on.

Miguel was sure that things were about to go from bad to worse; there was nothing to prevent the witches from sailing the enchanted boat to the moon, if they wished. Or perhaps they would discover him and turn him into a toad or a goat.

He pulled the tarp over his head, trembling and shaking like a fish cast out of the water.

When he next awoke, Miguel took some time before daring to stick his head outside the tarp and look around.

With a start, he realized that the witches were gone. The boat was no longer floating above the water. It wasn't sailing, either. It lay stranded, listing slightly, on a sandy stretch of beach. With an audible sigh of relief, he cast aside the tarp and took stock of his situation.

A quick look around informed him that he was not on São Miguel, his home. Instead, he had washed up on the sands of Praia Formosa, on the island of Santa Maria.

He shook his head clear, climbed out of the boat, and staggered a step or two.

At that precise moment he came face to face with Ana Sofia Moura.

Now and then, Ana Sofia enjoyed a solitary stroll along the beach before going to work. She especially liked to come to the beach after a good storm, and the previous night had brought the year's fiercest storm so far. She loved to be the first to make footsteps in the still wet sand, as if no one had ever walked there before, knowing that a few hours later those same footsteps would be gone, as if they never were. Sometimes she found something that had washed up on the sand or the rocks: a shell, a piece of wood, or a plastic bottle—none with notes inside—but this was the first time she had found a man.

Ana Sofia worked at the village council office in nearby Almagreira. She looked to be in her twenties, if one was forced to assign an age to her. Slender, with fair hair and skin, she possessed a remarkable face. Within the depths of her eyes, eons swirled like water coursing through the deepest wells. Bright rays of childhood sparkled in the expression of her lips. Wit, the joyousness of life, wisdom, playfulness, and a touch of mischief were revealed in her smile. A radiance emanated from Ana Sofia's every pore; a radiance that Miguel felt as much as he saw.

Ana Sofia watched as Miguel climbed out of his boat. She was surprised, not startled, and instantly curious.

"Good morning," he said, in a voice rough as the surf.

"I've never seen a man washed up by a storm," she said.

"Huh?"

"You're not from here." It was a statement, not a question.

"I'm from Povoação. São Miguel." He didn't know what else to say. He couldn't very well tell her about the witches. He scratched his head. "I must have drifted off course."

"Have you eaten?" she said. "You look like you've had a rough night."

Miguel smoothed out his shirt and jacket, which of course he had slept in. He was certain he looked a sight. He hadn't eaten since the day before, and was now quite hungry. "Is there a place to eat here?"

She led him to her car and drove to Vila do Porto. They ate in a café. She phoned her office to say she would be late—a family emergency. Miguel ate some rolls and fresh cheese, and had several cups of coffee. Ana Maria just had coffee.

He couldn't take his eyes off her. For all he knew this woman was a lingering manifestation the witches had conjured the night before. He swallowed several times, clearing his throat as if to speak but, when he opened his mouth, nothing came out. He stared at her as if she had appeared out of the sea foam.

Ana Sofia smiled. Miguel tried looking at her hair, but then wondered what it felt like, what it smelled like. So he looked instead at her clothes. She wore a red print blouse, a cream sweater, and slacks. His eyes widened at the sight of her breasts. He quickly turned away. He stared at her arm resting on the table. He felt his head spin. The witches, he thought. They must have left a spell on me. An enchantment. Either that, or the woman who sat before him was an apparition.

"I guess I should get back," he said. Although it was the last thing he wanted to say. He wanted to ask her about her life, to sit and talk for hours.

He began to reach for his wallet, but Ana Maria had already paid the bill. He realized he hadn't even brought his wallet. He had no money.

"Thank you," he stammered, his face and neck turning bright red.

There was an awkward pause, a long moment in which everything seemed to hang in suspension. Again, he gazed at her delicate hands, which rested on the table, then reached to touch her empty coffee cup and saucer.

"I'll take you back to your boat," Ana Sofia said. "You can sail back home."

He nodded.

When they reached Praia Formosa, Ana Sofia didn't drop him off and leave. She walked with him back to the boat. A fine rain began falling as they walked.

Miguel touched the side of the boat, as if he weren't sure whether it was real, or might vanish like a mirage. He reached in and pulled back the tarp.

"My God," he shouted, in astonishment.

Ana Sofia gazed down at the hull of the boat. "Fish," she said, with a shrug.

"I didn't fish last night," he said. "And I have never brought in that much fish. Ever."

There were several very large baskets filled high with fish, but of such a variety as he had never seen before.

"That's a lot?" she asked, innocently.

"More than I see in a whole week of fishing."

The sun broke through the clouds and shone where they stood.

It had to be the witches, he thought. But *why*?

"Ah, the witches are dancing!" Ana Sofia suddenly exclaimed.

"*What*?" Miguel said. He stared at her. Did she know?

"Look," she pointed up at the sky.

He looked, dumbfounded.

"You know what they say when it's raining and sunny—that the witches are dancing."

It was indeed sunny, and raining too.

Ana Sofia watched as Miguel pushed his boat out beyond the waves, set the small sail, and steered himself back to Povoação.

Miguel waved at her and Ana Sofia waved back. She wondered if she would ever see him again.

Miguel sat in his boat, filled to the gunwales with fish, and watched as the woman he'd met on the beach after a night with the witches grew smaller, not looking away until she had disappeared from view.

A week later Miguel found cause to return to Santa Maria. He made another trip shortly after that, and several more during the next few months. A year later Miguel and Ana Sofia were engaged.

The night before they were married, Miguel finally told her about the witches. She listened quietly, nodded, and smiled.

Ana Sofia didn't say a word. Miguel wasn't sure she believed him, but ever after, whenever the subject came up, Ana Sofia was quick to note that it was the witches who had brought them together.

The Thief of Santa Inês

IN THE TINY AZOREAN VILLAGE OF SANTA INÊS, ON THE ISLAND OF PICO, no one could remember when anyone had ever been accused of stealing more than a chicken or a knife. Nor did anyone remember when the cell in the city hall had ever been inhabited, other than by an occasional drunk. However, Sonia de Melo was a thief who stole from everyone, and worse yet, stole what she could not be arrested for. She took what wasn't hers and coveted these ill-gotten acquisitions, guarding them as if they were more precious than her own children.

When Dona Maria de Neves had a miscarriage, who stole every moment of pain and agony from the poor woman? Who broke out in a sweat, crying and swearing? Sonia de Melo. And when old man Norigudo got his leg amputated it was Sonia again who, as if drunk on *aguardente*, yelled and kicked up such a fuss.

Sonia's husband, José Vasco, struggled to comfort and soothe the poor woman, who suffered every calamity known to the islands, though he never understood how or why she suffered these terrible ills.

He wistfully remembered the young woman he had fallen in love with. She had always been a sensitive, even passionate girl, but it wasn't until some time after their marriage that she had become obsessed with pain and suffering as if these were all there was to be gotten from life.

People who used to visit the house, who always began their visits by running down the list of their latest ailments—"Ah, Dona Sonia, this pain I have here in my back"—who compared their every ache or symptom, trying their best to outdo one another, soon kept their problems to themselves, afraid of disclosing anything to Sonia, who would make any illness her own.

She was plagued with fevers, chills, aches and pains; she felt betrayed, unloved, lonely, and endured numerous *saudades*—that famed Portuguese longing, an intense yearning, a fond remembrance laden with a melancholy—for things she couldn't even name.

"She's nothing but a hypochondriac," her neighbors said. "There is nothing the matter with her. No one could have so much sorrow."

It happened over and over. Whenever someone suffered, Sonia stole the suffering from them. When lovers broke up she moaned in heartache, unable to eat or sleep for many days and nights. And when Maria Teresa went into a labor that lasted thirty-six hours, nobody had to be told that Sonia was the one who screamed with pain all day and night, clutching her bedclothes and nearly dying from the ordeal.

"Why must she take our pain?" Joana Maria dos Santos da Purificação asked. Joana Maria had been diagnosed, by several specialists, as suffering from an incurable melancholia, but that distinction had quickly been snatched away from her—even before she'd had a chance to relish it—by Sonia's symptoms, which, of course, proved far worse than Joana Maria's had ever been.

"Isn't there enough suffering in the world for everybody?" Joana's friend Hortênsia asked. "She has to take ours?"

"Is she so special?" asked Joana Maria. "Does she think she is a saint simply because she can steal our sufferings?"

Some villagers weren't disturbed by Sonia's excesses. "Good," they said. "Let her suffer. Better her than us." Many of them, however, were envious as well as suspicious, feeling that not being able to suffer was no life at all. Since life offered but little, they had learned to cling fiercely to what they had.

Of course, some people were more pious than others, and such distinctions were carefully noted. If one was capable of enduring more than their share of pains and troubles, in the name of God, then certainly God would reward that person for their piety, if not in this life then in the next.

The villagers disagreed on exactly how and when this state of affairs had come about. Some insisted that Sonia had always been this way, and that things only worsened after marriage and children. Still others claimed that Sonia had been a normal girl and some mysterious event had transformed her life, leaving her forever blighted.

"What could it be?" her neighbors asked. "What terrible sin turned Sonia de Melo into a thief?"

Sonia's great-grandmother had been known throughout the island as a powerful *feiticeira*, or sorceress, and it was thought by some that Sonia was now paying for the evil eyes which her great-grandmother, Maria Ernesta de Oliveira Moreno, had put on many of the villagers. Or that Sonia had attempted to practice her great-grandmother's arts before she was ready, and the magic had backfired.

No one could say exactly how Sonia stole their pain and their anguish, or how her suffering so eclipsed that of the true victims of misfortune that they were left incapable of feeling anything other than a disquieting numbness. But no one doubted the events that took place, and it wasn't long before people began to shun her.

"Look, up the road there. Isn't that Sonia?" Maria de Fátima said.

"Quick, then, let's go this way. She won't see us," said her neighbor Maria Teresa.

One night Maria Palmeira's husband was caught in a storm out in his boat. Sonia's cries and wails were heard throughout the night, from one end of town to the other. When the storm cleared there was no sign of the boat or the man.

Sonia spent each of the next nine days in church, weeping as she walked back and forth between her house, pulling her hair out in clumps, pinching her skin until it bruised and bled—more tears than anyone had ever seen. Meanwhile, Maria Palmeira didn't—indeed couldn't—shed a single tear.

Sonia's husband, José Vasco, helped nurse her back to health. "We need you, Sonia. Think of the children."

She burst into tears.

"What's wrong?" her husband asked.

"I am thinking of the children. Oh, the terrible lives they will live. Just think how miserable they will be."

Vasco left the house exhausted. He spent the evening at the café with a glass of *aguardente* that refilled itself every time he turned around, thanks to the kindness and sympathy of his friend Pedro, behind the counter. Pedro watched Vasco drink. "Poor man," he mumbled. "He is cursed. No one deserves such a fate."

Vasco drank as if the solution to all his problems lay lost somewhere in the bottom of his glass.

"Don't worry," Pedro assured him. "Things will improve." Pedro didn't have the heart to repeat the general belief that things couldn't possibly get much worse for the man.

José Vasco had worked hard, had always worked hard. Year after year, he waited patiently for something better to come along. One day he awoke and realized that nothing better was going to appear: it was too late—things weren't going to change. He had what little he had and would never have more than that.

The other villagers gossiped among themselves, never at a loss to discuss the latest of Sonia's symptoms and the unfortunate state of her poor family.

"Vasco should leave that woman," Joana Maria said. "After all, he is a decent man."

"He should find himself another wife, is what he should do," Hortênsia said. "Then Sonia de Melo would finally have something to cry about!"

"Yes," the others agreed. "The poor man, and those children."

"Have you seen the daughter?" José Pacheco asked. "Maria Antónia. There is something about that child."

"Strange, you mean."

"Yes, her eyes."

"They are a mystery, indeed."

The entire village was afraid of little Maria Antónia's magnificent eyes. They were of indeterminate color, and churned and swirled with immeasurable depths that clearly contained more than the whole world.

"I only hope and pray that she doesn't take after the mother," said Maria da Conceição.

Prayers were quickly offered to the Virgin Mother on behalf of Vasco and the children.

Vasco stumbled home drunk late that night. He fell into bed already asleep.

In the morning he was awakened by the groans of his wife. "My head," she said. "I feel like someone beat me with a stick."

She had stolen his hangover.

Without speaking a word, Vasco crawled out of bed and left the house.

He went to farm his fields, though the soil there was better suited to harvesting rocks than potatoes or wheat. He checked his vineyards: they too were poor. There wouldn't be much wine this year. Even the few cows he owned were thin and didn't offer much in the way of milk. All in all, it looked like another miserable year.

Vasco came home that evening, saddened and dejected, until he noticed Sonia looking as though the whole world had fallen upon her shoulders. She stared at the wall and didn't even seem to realize that Vasco was there. She sighed and trembled with every breath she took.

"No dinner?" he asked. "Where are the children?"

She didn't answer, but continued staring. Vasco went and gathered the children together. He sent them down the road to his mother's house.

What could he do? His sons, Henrique and João, could stay with his uncle and Vasco's mother. And perhaps his little girl, Maria Antónia, could stay with Sonia's sister in Praia Negra, on the island of Faial. Sonia's sister, at least, appeared to be normal. Vasco shrugged.

"Every family," he said, "seems to have one who's crazy and one who is not, one who is beautiful and one who is ugly. God does as he sees fit."

It might be for the best. After all, the children had been forced to keep more than one sickness to themselves, fearful, knowing they couldn't possibly compete with their mother, who resented any illness or affliction that troubled someone else, including members of her own family.

Then he went to speak with Sonia. "Maybe I will go to Horta or Terceira, and look for work," he said.

Sonia looked at him, her eyes wide and moist with sadness. "Horta? I will be left alone? The children, too?" She fanned herself, exclaiming, "Ah, I feel faint."

Vasco left the room. He grabbed his coat and hat, which he normally used only on feast days, and went out.

Vasco wandered the streets like a sleepwalker, day and night, stopping off at taverns, leaving, stumbling up one road and down another. One day a shopkeeper in town stopped him and told him how sorry he was to hear that one of Vasco's sisters in America had fallen ill and died. It was the first that Vasco had heard of the news.

Vasco remained calm and composed. He chuckled to himself, thinking how Sonia would be in mourning at that moment for his sister, even though Sonia had never liked his sister in the first place.

Still laughing, Vasco began inflicting pain upon himself. If there was a rock in the road he intentionally tripped on it; if he passed a donkey that was known to bite or kick, he encouraged the beast to do its worst.

At first he wasn't sure whether these attempts at harming himself were working. But he heard some gossip, and finally began stopping by his house to see for himself. There was Sonia, each and every time, holding her foot, or her head, or her side, moaning. Vasco smiled, relieved. If he had hurt himself on the arm, there was a corresponding bruise, purple or reddish, upon Sonia's arm.

Satisfied, Vasco left in search of new ways in which to hurt himself.

The villagers thought poor Vasco had lost his mind. He was in terrible shape, covered with scrapes and bruises. Practically a day didn't go by when he didn't receive some new injury. Some people claimed to have seen him hitting himself, while others swore that he had begged them to hit him.

But it was his expression through all this that caused the most alarm in the villagers. No matter how badly he was hurt, his expression was one of utter contentment, of inexplicable peace, of joy.

Sonia suffered, as only she could. "Ah, *meu Deus*, my own children and husband have abandoned me. I am a forgotten and unloved woman!" Her neighbors heard her endless sighs, as she stared out her open windows, where she looked longingly up the same empty street, crying rivers of tears and bemoaning her plight. "I am forsaken."

During her husband's absence, Sonia became stricken and helpless, unable to do even the simplest things for herself. Each breath was a labor, every movement an ordeal.

Vasco subjected himself to every conceivable hardship, to all forms of abuse, to any possible method of pain or displeasure. He relished them all, savored every one with an unquenchable enthusiasm. No matter how bruised and battered, how sore or uncomfortable, he was filled with a newfound sense of satisfaction, knowing that back at home, his wife Sonia was suffering all his agonies.

Vasco stopped eating food. He slept outside in the cold, without any covering. He went about barefoot until his feet were raw and blistered.

And still, he wore a look of happiness, which was all the more disconcerting and unusual to the townspeople, because none of them could recall having seen Vasco laugh or smile before. "No," Gil Garante reflected. "He never used to smile. He never had anything to smile about." The others agreed.

Sonia's neighbors tried to inform her of Vasco's strange behavior, amid all her sufferings. "Dear Mother of God, now my husband has lost his mind!" she exclaimed.

One day Vasco stood on the edge of a cliff, waiting for death to take him.

He tried working his feet into a trick from which he wouldn't be able to back out, knowing he couldn't intentionally jump. Any fool knew that to kill oneself was a hell of a mortal sin; but an accident—well, now, that was another matter altogether. And what else could it be but a tragic accident if Vasco had a bit too much to drink, stumbled on the edge of the cliff, and drowned in the sea below?

But if he did drown, he thought, other things might go badly. He decided against taking the risk. He turned, ready to walk away, but then stumbled on a root and fell backwards, over the cliff to the sea below.

But Vasco was not falling—death, like everything else, was giving him the cold shoulder. He remembered the words of his grandmother, Dona Maria da Conceição: "No one ever dies on this island because they are all born dead. And all one can do is wait for that time which is not of being born or dying, but the birth of unbeing."

He floated up above the cliff, realizing that his grandmother had been right. He was a simple man who hadn't had much time to learn more than what was necessary for survival. Like most people who'd known her, he'd believed his grandmother was somewhat eccentric and her words wholly incomprehensible.

His grandmother had believed that life was itself a ridiculous predicament. Thus Vasco reasoned, if we are all born dead to begin with, well, then to live or die, does it make any difference? Once you are dead does it really matter that, for a few brief moments, you were alive? How does one weigh a lifetime against an awaiting eternity of oblivion? Death, after all, seemed to be the natural order of things, with life a mere afterthought, a momentary flicker of consciousness, no different from a dream, really.

Thus Vasco didn't fall and didn't die. Instead, he walked back to Santa Inês feeling very tired, longing for the time when he could at long last rest.

Sonia, never to be outdone, did the only thing she could do under the circumstances: she stole Vasco's death.

Such a terrible commotion rumbled up the narrow stone streets of the village, as word of Sonia's death made its way from house to house, to the cafés, the market, a restaurant or two. Even those working in the fields outside Santa Inês soon heard the news of how Sonia de Melo had suddenly gone to the angels.

This was how Vasco learned that his wife had passed away. He returned home greatly disturbed. Not only had Sonia taken his death by drowning, but he now felt all of his own pain and suffering once again. Sonia had escaped;

she was finally free of the troubles and burdens of her unhappy life. But he, Vasco, was without a wife and children, even poorer than he had been before, and suffering from all the pains and deprivations he had so recently endured.

∼∼∼

This is the story as it happened in the village of Santa Inês, on the island of Pico. But this isn't the end of the story. That didn't take place until seven years had gone by.

The funeral procession slowly and solemnly passed through the narrow streets of Santa Inês. They were finally going to bury Senhor José Vasco de Melo.

"There's no turning back now," José Pacheco said.

"He'll be put into the ground like anyone else," said Pedro, who owned the café. "This matter will be settled once and for all."

"Yes," said Joana Maria. "There'll be no more of this foolishness."

"Dead is dead," Hortênsia said.

"At last!" they all said at once.

Everybody attending the funeral had heard Vasco refer to himself as a dead man; "I died seven years ago," he said repeatedly, to anyone who would listen, even upon the last day he was alive. "I am simply waiting to die my true death." And so for seven long, dreary years, he had awaited this day.

The villagers all knew about Vasco's foiled attempt to jump from the cliff, and they knew as well that Sonia had stolen his death from him. For seven years they had watched a dead man who hadn't yet decided to give up the ghost. For seven long years half the village had treated him as if he were a ghost, and the other half as if nothing had happened, as if he were no different from the Vasco of old.

"What do we know of such things," they said. "For all we know he may live forever."

And then one day, without warning, he dropped dead. Gone! And what do you think? Did poor Vasco finally go to his long-awaited and much-needed rest? And what about Sonia? Who knows? However, rumor has it that she is busy stealing all of Vasco's heavenly pleasures—along with everyone else's—right this very moment.

The Newest Star

MARIO STARED, ENTRANCED, WHILE BEFORE HIS VERY EYES JOANA Medroso made her way down the hill, floating several inches off the ground. She looked no different from the other girls her own age, but Mario knew she wasn't like any of them.

Why, after all, did she have to admonish the birds and butterflies not to follow her, whenever she walked to town? When they were younger Joana had allowed Mario to visit her secret corner of the yard, where she had demonstrated a special way of charming spiders into building extraordinarily ornate webs, designs that she herself had helped to create.

No one could believe it when Joana Medroso had announced she would marry Joaquim, least of all Mario. He had watched her from near and far; somehow, he felt that she couldn't possibly go off and marry someone else, that the two of them were in some way linked, sharing a mystery that was merely waiting to work itself out, to reveal a wealth of new meanings—an unfolding and flowering of certain unspoken promises.

It had been two years since the wedding, but Mario still refused to recognize her husband's place. He would only call her Joana Medroso, never by Joaquim's family name. Joaquim, he insisted, was an impostor, a bum who hardly ever worked and who sponged off her parents. Joana deserved much better. And now that she had been unable to have a child, even after two years of marriage, he was sure it had something to do with their secret.

In all of Horta, and indeed in all the Azores, Mario knew there was not another girl like his Joana Maria.

Joana was only a couple of years older than Mario, yet she still treated him like a child. True, they had played games together while their mothers chatted, and it was not *so* long ago that she had shown him the hidden garden in the very back of her family's yard. Still, he'd had to bear the pain and shock of her marriage, though he couldn't quite imagine how it had happened. He had seen nothing between them. It must have been all her mother's doing.

Mario watched her move down the street, just as he had done numerous times. "*Bom dia*, Mariozinho," Joana said playfully, teasing, as he passed her, her dress like a light blue sail before his eyes. He wasn't a little boy anymore; he was fifteen now. Mario blushed, turning away for a moment, then looked after her. As always, he was struck speechless. Even in her kindness she could be cruel.

He finally found his voice, though it came out as no more than a whisper. "*Bom dia*, Joana." He refused to refer to her as *dona* or *senhora*, the way everyone else did.

She wore a dress that went past her knees and flared outward in a colorful sweep of flowers and vines. There was something almost wild and untamed about her, something that the animals recognized—as if she were one of them, not like the people she lived among.

He stood watching the bare part of her lower legs, her feet in tiny light shoes that tapped on the cobblestone street, her wide, curving hips, and the dress billowing recklessly in the warm wind of the afternoon.

He wished there was some way he could control his heartbeat; it beat rhythms he was wholly unused to, like the fast songs he sometimes heard from Brazil. It left him sweaty and struggling to catch his breath, almost as bad as the time his friend, Manuel, had hit him in the stomach.

She hardly ever took notice of him, as if he were still a little boy. But he knew far more than he had when they used to play together. He was grown up now; he had seen his uncle die, and a friend his own age had drowned. He had changed. He'd grown taller and stronger, and felt as if the lava that sometimes erupted from the mountain filled his veins instead of blood. And *she*? She was like the sea, restless and unpredictable.

Other girls wore dresses and walked by, but Joana held secrets within the folds of her skirt. He saw her pause to talk to a girlfriend. Her dress rippled and played in the breeze.

Waves.

Her dress seemed so full, so alive. He wondered if there was light that shone there, where her legs widened and met, joining the rest of her body.

Mario could see she was content, happy with her secret. Did she think of it as a mystery to protect? He had a vision of twilight in a garden.

He looked at her bottom, which had widened. It was not fat or even large, but there was so much beneath that dress: new uncharted worlds.

It was worse when he thought about her at night: then images would spring to mind of the exotic creatures which he envisioned lurking in that strange region, of the wild, changing topiary of secret hairs, the white sandy strand of her stomach, the tug of tides flowing, the echo of waves, and the whisper of something not yet spoken.

Whenever near her, he couldn't control the urge to reach over and touch her, to brush against her, even though it always left him feeling shaken and weak.

He had never seen her with any boyfriends, and he kept his feelings about her to himself. Everyone else thought she was odd, different. "She's a strange, moody child," people said. "A dreamy child." Her round face, pale in contrast with her long, almost black hair. Light gray eyes that sometimes mirrored the color of the horizon.

As Joana talked to her friends, Mario watched how she kept her hands at her sides, as though she had to constantly keep her dress from flying out. You could see it: furtive movements here and there, very quick, with the expertise of calm yet firm control. There was always a whirlwind blowing about her ankles and around her knees, lifting her skirt playfully.

She chatted freely, laughing and smiling, the words floating up out of her mouth as if they had wings of their own. And it didn't matter that he didn't know what she was saying; just to hear the musical sound of a word now and again was enough.

Then it was over, and all the girls left, leaving Mario standing alone, feeling lost.

Mario finally walked away and headed for home, eager to find out when he could go with his mother to visit the Medroso family—to see Joana smile and to breathe in her scent.

∼ ∼ ∼

Joana Medroso's family quietly settled down at the long table for supper. There were settings for ten, though only five were seated. The house felt both empty and hollow, as if a death had fallen upon the household. There was usually a bustle of neighbors and friends visiting for lunch or dinner, and in the evenings talking politics, or about the problems of the islands, the way Lisbon always took from the Azores but gave nothing in return, or gossiping about the other families of Horta. But people had been visiting less often of late, as Joana's inability to conceive had become more and more a topic of conversation and concern.

"This is not life," Joana's mother, Maria Conceição de Medroso, said in a shaky voice, "but a vale of tears." She looked heavenward and sighed. She was a large woman whose face drooped in a fixed look of sorrow. When she sighed her cheeks and double chin shook.

"What was that?" asked her husband. "Clichés? Another something you got out of one of your damned books?"

"Go ahead, swear and make light of our misery. So what if we are the laughingstock? What do you care that the whole world knows of our shame?"

"Mother, please," Joana said, stammering.

"Shame, flame. I don't care what these fools think or say behind my back." Senhor Medroso was a silver-haired man in his late sixties, who, despite his small frame, was taut and muscular. He leaned forward as he spoke, and appeared to be on the verge of vaulting across the table.

"It is not asking so much, is it? My only daughter, to have one child? One offspring? What is a woman to do?"

"Mother!"

Conceição's son-in-law, Joaquim, cleared his throat.

"Well, aren't you going to say something?" Joana said.

"To be married two empty years," Conceição continued. "Lord, what a burden."

Joana got up from the table, threw her napkin down on her chair, and stormed out of the room. Joaquim continued to sit, slurping his soup.

"That girl's temper is only going to make matters worse. How can someone so temperamental possibly conceive?"

"In the middle of my meal do I have to listen to this kind of talk?" Senhor Medroso shouted. "Enough is enough!"

"Just look at our table. It's half empty. Why do you think no one comes here to see us?"

Joaquim wiped his mouth on his napkin and helped himself to the platter of meat.

DARRELL KASTIN

"So much the better. Let them stay at home. I don't need to see a bunch of nosy old windbags anyway."

"We should pack up and move far away, where no one will know."

Joaquim reached across the table for a roll.

Conceição seemed to suddenly take notice of him. "And you," she said, pointing. "What are you doing about the situation?"

"I try, senhora. I cannot work miracles." He reached for another roll.

"Bah! Why, dear Mother of God, why? I will take her once again to the padre, tonight. We will light another candle."

∼ ∼ ∼

Later that evening Conceição sat knitting her twentieth baby sweater, for the child that never came, and listening to the radio. Joana read. The men had gone out for the night.

"I know how it is," Conceição said suddenly. "Sometimes it is very difficult, but worth it after all in the end. Trust me."

Joana groaned.

"After all, there are sacrifices and there are sacrifices. It won't work from prayers alone."

"Yes, Mother."

"You must try harder, dear. Believe with all your soul. Pray each night to Santo António that he might help you to be with child."

Joana nodded.

"Think of nothing more than the blessed event of giving birth, of the good for the family, the honor of being one of God's vessels, of the rewards, and God will see you're paid for the trouble."

"Good night, Mother."

The next morning Conceição walked to the market. She had long ago decided that no one but her was to be trusted with the shopping. She wound her way around the stands briskly, avoiding the looks of the other women. She didn't bother to squeeze the various fruits and vegetables, frowning with displeasure, or to turn her nose up at the selection of chicken and meat, as she normally did. She pushed her way through, roughly grabbing the food that she picked without much care, haphazardly.

She set her jaw, then muttered a litany of curses and invocations. "Why, why must I have to suffer this ignoble fate, this burden? Has the world turned against me? Just look at their faces, talking behind our backs. I hope their cows run dry, and may their children grow up simple! It's a sign; God is upset about something. Perhaps in his infinite wisdom he has decided to put an end to our family once and for all. Why? What have we done?"

She stopped by the church and prayed fervently.

~ ~ ~

Mario and his mother showed up at the house before dinner. Conceição appeared flustered when they walked in. They were the first guests to stop by in over a week. "Oh, it's so good to see you, Dona Lucia." She rushed up and kissed Senhora Sena, then hugged her warmly, her flabby arms shaking. "Ana, come take her coat. What is the matter with you?" The maid hurried in and took Senhora Sena's coat and Mario's jacket.

Conceição patted Mario's head. "Mario, you've certainly grown into such a handsome boy." She smiled and clasped her hands together.

She led them into the dining room. "Please, sit down. I'm so glad you stopped by."

"How is Joana?" Senhora Sena asked.

"Oh, she's in a state. We all are. I just don't know what to do any more. I'm worried sick."

"It is such a terrible shame," Senhora Sena said, reaching over to touch Conceição's arm.

"*Sim*. We've tried everything, but nothing has helped."

Senhor Medroso came into the room, followed by Joana and Joaquim. They were startled to see Senhora Sena. "*Boa tarde*, Dona Lucia," Senhor Medroso said dryly. Joana and Joaquim kissed her, muttering, "*Boa tarde*, Dona Lucia," then sat down at their seats.

Ana began to bring the food into the room; everyone sat and ate in silence.

Mario had sat down in the seat next to Joana, and he looked at her to see if she heard his heart beating. She didn't appear to notice.

He ate little, and once he swore he felt her dress rub up against his leg.

Mario looked at her and his stomach hardened. Why had she married Joaquim? Anyone could see she was miserable. And he was just a lazy oaf.

After the meal Senhora Sena took Conceição aside. "I have something for Joana," she said.

"Oh? Something for the problem?" Conceição asked, growing excited.

"Yes. I was given some herbs by Senhora Fagundes. And Senhora Silva said the wings of this butterfly, here," she handed Conceição an envelope, "that these are very good for conception."

"Butterfly wings?" Conceição said.

"The wings of a very special butterfly, senhora, one that lives at the top of Pico and no where else."

"Thank you, Senhora Sena. Who knows? I hope this solves the problem."

"I'm sure something will happen, you'll see."

"Mario. You're so quiet these days. Almost grown up."

As Mario and Senhora Sena left, Conceição pleaded with Mario's mother to come back soon, to not stay away so long, for her house was theirs.

∼ ∼ ∼

Mario's backyard bordered a field where a neighbor often let his cows graze. On the other side of the field there was a row of tall trees, and behind that the Medrosos' yard.

One day Mario walked through the field, which was now empty. The sun was overhead, the air warm and still, heavy with the sweet pungent smell of the cows. He strolled up close to the tree behind Joana's yard. He'd used to climb this tree, to sit on one of its high branches, watching the birds and staring off at Pico in the distance.

He walked between the trees, thinking of Joana and wondering if his mother was right, that the herbs and other things would finally make Joana pregnant.

He heard a girl's laugh. He moved through the trees and pushed aside the vines to peer into the yard.

Joana sat on a blanket. She was watching a glass ballerina twirl on the blanket. A glass star hung in the air several feet above the dancer. The star caught the sunlight as it turned and reflected colors. Joana laughed and clapped her hands.

It was Joana's garden, where they used to play. Where the two of them had been constant companions, when they were both still children, before she had grown up.

Joana's dress, spread out around her, covered half the blanket. A tiny creature crawled out from under the edge of her dress. Mario had never seen anything like it. It moved slowly, was rounded like a shell, and seemed to be

THE NEWEST STAR

made of glass, though it was furrowed and had a purplish tint. He strained to see where it had come from, but all he could see was the edge of Joana's dress.

Joana reached over and petted the creature, which began singing, making a sound like a music box.

"You sweet thing," Joana said.

Mario felt light. He wanted to fly, to take her up into the air with him, to float on the gentle wings of her dress. She hadn't really changed at all. This must be part of the secret. This creature was part of the magic she used, and perhaps it kept her from having babies.

~ ~ ~

Mario returned to the garden every chance he got, where he'd watch Joana from his hiding place in the trees. Sometimes she danced around the blanket while he could only stare, breathless, as she swayed in the sunlight and fragrance. She twirled and moved in the isolated garden, as her dress rose in the air, showing her knees and, occasionally, the pale, creamy skin of her thighs.

Other times she would sit and watch the creatures perform, or simply lie there, looking up at the sky or picking the petals off a flower.

One day, as Joana danced, humming a pretty melody, a bird flew out from under her dress. It was small, not quite the size of Mario's fist, and bright blue and yellow. It was the prettiest bird Mario had ever seen.

The bird circled Joana, flapping its wings and singing, its birdsong dense with the sound of wind rushing through the island's thick groves of trees, or of water when the stream was full.

Joana lay down and appeared to go to sleep. The bird flew in a descending spiral and slowly came down to rest on the blanket beside her.

Mario suddenly wanted the bird. What would it hurt? He would just borrow it. She could have it back later. She kept everything to herself, so secret, and he only wanted to be a part of that world, her world, even if just for a little while.

He moved cautiously between the trees, careful not to step on the twigs. He sneaked up to the blanket and reached out his hand. Her dress was so close, but he couldn't risk waking her.

Mario grabbed the bird and made his way back to the cover of the trees. Then he kept going, past the trees and through the field, back to his own yard.

He held the bird in the pocket of his jacket. When he got to his back door, he took the bird out and let it rest on his palm.

Mario entered his house and went upstairs to his room. He placed the bird in the bottom drawer of his dresser.

∼∼∼

Mario was scared to go back to the garden, though he knew Joana hadn't seen him, and couldn't know he had the bird. Still, he was afraid to look at her.

He spent most of his time in his room, taking the bird out of the drawer and trying to get it to fly. The bird, he'd found, wasn't real, but made of glass like the other things he'd seen, even down to the feathers, which were thin transparent layers of glass, tinted yellow and blue. But for some reason the bird refused to fly, and after an hour or so he would put it back in the drawer.

He heard from his mother that Joana was behaving differently, though nobody said why. Perhaps, Mario thought, the herbs and butterfly wings his mother had given Senhora Medroso were the cause.

Days later he saw Joana. He hardly recognized her. She walked listlessly down the *avenida* that stretched along the waterfront. Her dress hung limp, as if it was wet. It had no life at all. The wind blew, but the dress hardly moved.

Joana had changed. She seemed old and sad. What had happened? Mario wondered.

The bird too lay lifeless on his floor whenever he took it out. Its colors appeared to be fading as well.

He saw her several times over the next few days, but there was nothing of the old, familiar Joana. He couldn't stand it. He wanted her to laugh and dance the way she always had before, to smile and show the sparkle of her eyes. He longed to hear her singing and playing in her secret garden, but when he went to her yard she wasn't there anymore.

That night Mario took the bird out of the drawer and petted its smooth glass feathers. It didn't make a sound. He peered at its green eyes. "I'll take you back."

He went out the back door and ran to Joana's house. He was relieved to find her window open, and aimed, about to toss the bird through. He would make everything all better. "Go back," he whispered to the bird. He would watch Joana play tomorrow as he hid in the trees.

He drew his arm back and threw the bird straight up to the window, but instead of flying inside it curved and sailed higher, above the house.

It paused for a brief moment, turned, and was no longer a bird but the glass star he had seen Joana with that first day. The star shot forward into the night—a streak of bright light across the sky. Mario remembered how his uncle in Praia Negra had always said a shooting star meant a new baby had come into the world. It hung there among the other stars, glittering and winking, as Mario stood and gasped.

The next day his mother told him he had to go with her to shop for some material, so she would have something made by the time Joana's baby arrived.

The Secret Place

*So for centuries the peak has stood, sublime and quiet,
but even now, its crown is warm; there, unexpected at that altitude,
there are warmth-loving species of butterflies.*
BERNARD VENABLES ~ *Baleia! Baleia! Whale Hunters of the Azores*

EMILIO BORGES DISEMBARKED AT THE WHARF IN MADALENA AND walked stiffly to the bus, struggling to hide the pain that made him move with such difficulty. He carried a bag filled with a change of clothing and other belongings, from which a butterfly net protruded.

He sniffed the air appreciatively as he walked away from the boat.

Ah, it is good to be back on Pico once again.

Emilio stepped onto the waiting bus. He nodded at the driver and sat down, then took out his handkerchief and wiped the sweat from his forehead. He ignored the driver and the others on the bus who turned to look, perhaps curious as to why he, an old man, was carrying a butterfly net.

Emilio glanced out the window toward Pico, but the mountain was covered with clouds. He thanked God that his first venture off the island was finally over. It would be his last, no matter what anyone said. He was sure of that. He'd had enough of doctors. And boats. Though he had lived his whole life on an island, he was a man of the land, of the mountain that was Pico, not of the ocean.

The bus quickly filled, then started the half-hour trip to Santo António, winding along the narrow road which circuited the island. He stared out the window, refusing to look at the other passengers, though he had seen one or two neighbors board the bus. He looked out at the green fields and the dense foliage of the checkerboard gardens, closed off by black walls of volcanic rock—walls that hid what lay inside, the way his body had hidden the disease for so long.

I won't sit helpless and wait for death. Doctors would rather have you crawl into a grave and be finished with it.

The bus dropped Emilio off in nearby Santa Luzia. He continued on foot down the road toward his home in the neighboring village of Santo António. Two of the villagers, Maria Inês and Isabel Fagundes, had scurried off the bus before him. They stood gathering their parcels and bags.

"Poor man," they said, shaking their heads, watching their silent neighbor make his way, step by painful step, toward his home.

The women waved when he looked at them.

Too weak to wave back, you old busybodies.

"What does he have in that bag, I wonder?" Isabel Fagundes said.

"He looks like a ghost," Maria Inês said, then moved her lips in a silent prayer, as she crossed herself.

"As if he can't see or hear us," Isabel said.

"Poor Maria Alice."

Emilio managed to smile at the thought of two women who couldn't possibly understand what he was doing with a butterfly net. He kept looking over toward Pico to see if the summit had broken through its shroud, but observed that it was still hiding its face.

"Only two days separate us," he said to the mountain. "Then, we will be together, eh? You, me, and the butterflies."

At last Emilio reached his home. He took out his kerchief and wiped the sweat from his forehead, then carefully folded the kerchief again and put it back in his pocket. His every breath came with a struggle. He waited a moment before entering the house.

Maria Alice had her hands full. She had soup on the stove and a dish of *bacalhau* on the table. Manuel was still out in the fields; he had grown into a fine, strong man. Antónia helped her mother with the meal. Antónia's child, Dionísio, had recently been born, and Emilio was pleased to be a grandfather. Maria Alice nearly dropped the food when she saw her husband enter the house.

"Emilio! What are you doing here? Back so soon?" She rushed up to him, and peered at his face. "What is wrong? What happened?"

Maria had an uncanny ability to detect the truth, as well as a fine nose for deception. Emilio knew he couldn't lie to her, and knew that by looking at him she would suspect the worst. Maria didn't have to state with words that he looked terrible.

"What did the doctors say?" she asked.

He didn't answer. She had fought fiercely to go with him to Terceira, but he had refused, insisting she stay home—he had wanted to go alone. He put down the bag and went to the cupboard. He took down the bottle of *aguardente*, poured a glassful and gulped it down. He poured another glassful and sat at the table.

"Well?" Maria Alice said. "What did they tell you?"

"Nothing," he said finally. He knew he had to tell her now. He took a deep breath. "I am going to climb Pico. I decided on the boat back from Terceira."

"You are going to do what?"

He sat back as his wife stared at him in disbelief. He might as well have said that he was going to the moon. "I will climb Pico."

"I can't believe my ears," she said, raising her hands with her palms up, the way that had always made him smile. "Why? What about the doctors?"

"I'm through with all that. The cancer is everywhere, and I am an old man. There's nothing they can do."

"Maybe you should go to some other doctors," Maria Alice said, softening her voice to a more conciliatory and persuasive tone. "We could go to San Miguel, see a specialist. They will do something, no?"

"There is nothing the doctors can do now but quicken the work God has already started. No, I will not go to any specialists. I have only one wish and that is to climb the mountain."

Maria puffed herself up, the way she did when she was angry, and folded her arms over her chest.

"You've never climbed Pico in all your life," she said. "It makes no sense. Why should you do this? Why now?"

"Because I want to."

"Who will go with to guide you?"

"No one. I must go alone."

"Dear God, save us! My poor husband has lost his mind. An old man, and he is going to go off on a crazy adventure and get himself killed!"

Emilio smiled, "She's worried about a dying man getting killed."

She ignored his comment, then noticed the butterfly net sticking out of Emilio's bag. "What is this?" she said.

"A net, to catch butterflies with," Emilio said.

"A what?"

"Listen woman," he said. "I met a man in Terceira, called himself a naturalist. He told me that at the top of Pico there are butterflies that can be found nowhere else. They live by the warmth of the crater. There and only there."

"So?"

"So, I want to see this butterfly."

The next day the whole village discussed the news that the dying man, Emilio, had lost his senses, and was going off to chase wild butterflies.

Emilio's oldest friend, Luís, who owned the café, tried to talk him out of his plan.

"There's nothing up there, old man," Luís said. "It's cold. Too high. Nothing grows up there, and nothing could live up there."

"How do you know?" Emilio asked. "Have you climbed up there to see? The naturalist told me that the warmth of the volcano keeps the butterflies alive."

"I don't need to go up there to know he was pulling your leg, Emilio. He's probably laughing right now, a good joke to tell an old man, yes?"

"It was no joke, Luís. The man had pictures. He showed me one he had caught, too. I am going up to see for myself."

Luís stared at his friend, a stubborn man who wouldn't listen to reason. "Look, Emilio," he said. "It's only a mountain. Leave it be. It was there before us and it will remain long after we are gone."

Emilio finished the drink Luís had proffered.

"Just a mountain, you say." Emilio spoke with finality. "We put ourselves into the soil here, our sweat and hard work. Just like our parents and grandparents before us. This is where we will all be buried. The mountain is part of us, just as we are part of the mountain. We are like the black stones of Pico."

Luís sighed. "So why climb? Pico is difficult. It's dangerous. People fall, they die."

"Because this butterfly has found a secret place where there are no others. It lives there alone, and perhaps it can only live in that one place. Anyway, I've decided I want to see them for myself before I die."

"This mountain is not for someone to go climb alone," Luís insisted. He mentioned the various people who had disappeared while attempting to climb Pico over the years, scientists and even experienced climbers who had gotten lost or fallen. "There are too many dangers," Luís said. Fog or clouds that came up without warning; *furnas* or craters that one could stumble into and fall hundreds of feet; the treacherous steep slopes.

"I've heard all that," Emilio said, waving away the so-called dangers. "People lose their way because they think they can conquer the mountain, right? But me, I go with a purpose, a search."

It was impossible. Emilio wouldn't listen. Not to his friends, not to Father Silva after Sunday Mass. He was going.

"Think of your wife and family," Father Silva said. "If God had meant for men to climb mountains—and you, an old man already. You are sick. Here is where you belong, with your family, your friends."

But nothing could shake Emilio's desire.

On the second night after his return from Terceira, Emilio kissed his sleeping children and grandchild good-bye. He walked out of the house, his traveling bag weighed down with some food, a jug of water, and a heavy rusted chain he had purchased for next to nothing from Claudio, the mechanic. He also carried the butterfly net that the naturalist had kindly given him, after Emilio had told the man that he too would climb Pico and find the butterflies that could live nowhere else.

"Can't you at least go when it's light?" Maria Alice pleaded. "Soon there will be rain, or perhaps snow. You could freeze up there."

"No. It is at night that the mountain bares its face. The clouds come with the sunrise." He kissed Maria Alice good-bye and held her briefly. "I will come back tomorrow." He started walking down the road.

"*Butterflies!*" he heard her say as he walked off. "What will I tell the children?"

"Tell them to look up at the mountaintop," he shouted. "If the weather is clear perhaps they will see me dancing with the butterflies."

The moon was full and Pico stood out, a dark tower jutting into the night, more felt than seen. Emilio was accompanied up the mountain by the sound his shoes made as they ground against the volcanic rock. On the side of the road he found a long, sturdy branch to use as a walking stick.

He climbed steadily, pausing now and again to rest or drink a bit of water. Up ahead the dark mountain loomed, always there, larger than life.

I'm coming, my friend. You don't seem so dangerous, so terrible. Just a mountain, eh?

It was true that over the years people had lost their way and disappeared, never to be seen again. But he had lived and worked his whole life here. Surely the mountain knew him as well as he knew the mountain.

He quickly left behind the houses and people, the cows, the patches of woods. Then it was only Emilio and the naked mountain. He listened to the wind rush down the slope—making a low, mournful howl as the air sang through the ravines and over the *furnas*, like blowing air across a bottle top.

"Ah, Pico is breaking wind," Maria Alice would have said. Emilio chuckled.

The path was steep and wound its way in a series of sharp switchbacks. He heard the sound of his breathing and occasionally rocks falling. The air was dry and smelled of the volcano, which slept, though no one knew when it might awaken. Now and then there had been rumbles, earthquakes.

He pushed himself to go farther, to ignore the thinning air and the steep passes, fearing that if he stopped, he might not be able to continue.

Emilio set himself landmarks to use as goalposts.

I will walk to that jutting rock up ahead before I stop. Then, after, to that crest, or that bend in the trail.

After a couple of hours he stopped and sat down to rest. He picked out the sharp stones that had lodged in the soles of his thin shoes and wiped the abrasions on his hands with a handkerchief.

You may have sharp teeth, mountain, but don't think that will stop me. I will not be turned back so easily.

Already he was tired, the climb more difficult than he had foreseen, and his body weaker, always weaker.

The lights from Faial, across the channel, blinked at him in the distance; he saw their ghosts on the dark surface of the water. He also could make out scattered lights on the island of São Jorge. Up at the top, the naturalist had said, you could see the others too: Terceira, Graciosa, almost all of the Azores with one glance. Up where the butterflies lived, hovering around the warm mountaintop; where steam escaped through cracks, steam from the very heart of the mountain.

Emilio took out some bread and a slice of meat, then ate, looking down at the world below.

It is so wide. Up here you can see there is so much nothingness out there.
The wind blew, low and mournful.
Such a sad voice you have, mountain.

After half an hour he continued walking. The paths were steep and treacherous, along cliffs and over rocks where there was poor footing and barely anything to hold on to.

Go on, make it difficult. You won't stop me. What are you hiding up there, eh?
He whistled a tune and wished he had better eyesight.
Ah, it's cold. Though thank God for the full moon. That and the fact that the skies are as clear as they have been in ages. There are not even birds up here.

His legs began to ache. The satchel felt heavier with each step, slowing him down.

This is nothing, too. Old bones, a tired body, but I have the strength to finish this. That is important. To have the will to make this climb.

Emilio kept moving. He told himself it was just around the next turn; one more ridge, and he would soon be there. Where many people half his age couldn't make it—where the scientist from the continent had found the butterfly that lived in its secret place.

He pushed himself onward, pressing down on his knees, forcing them to take another step. His breath came quickly and cut through his throat, his lungs.

Not too far. Keep going old man. You can't stop, now!

The mountain stood by, silent, imposing. On occasion, Emilio's feet would slip on the rocks, and he would hug the mountain closer. *What it must be to be as old as you are, eh, mountain? You do not die, like an old man. How many have you killed, I wonder?*

The sky began to lighten. Dawn was breaking. Looking down, he saw the enormous shadow the mountain cast upon the surface of the ocean. Still, the volcano rose before him, its peak beyond reach, as if for each step he took the summit moved farther away.

How can butterflies live in such a place? There are no trees or plants. Could the man have lied, like Luís said? Why would he tell me if it wasn't true? Did he think I would never climb to find out, that it was safe to tell an old fool like me there was something here when there wasn't? Maybe I was crazy to do this.

He paused and glanced at the ocean as the sun rose. Perhaps, he thought, the clouds will come. A storm could come without warning to the mountain. He pushed on, determined to reach the top, though the pain made his movements difficult.

Emilio strained, using his arms and hands against the rocks, to get past them, to pull himself up and over. He looked down but could no longer see much below, only the sea, which appeared so calm, so smooth. He smiled happily; he was with God now.

Maybe the mountain is God's big toe.

The trail wound its way around the edge of the mountain, then cut back into sheltered ground, so unlike the rest of Pico, which was barefaced. Emilio headed for that spot, frantic to reach his goal.

Ah, it is like a nest there in the mountain, a good spot for me to find shelter.

Inside the cut, the wind was quieter and the air was warmer. He could see the peak jutting up ahead of him. The top was very near.

He waved his arms at the cone of the volcano. "Hey, look! I made it, mountain. What do you think now?"

He put the heavy satchel down and suddenly felt weightless; even his clothes, which flapped in the breeze, seemed heavier than he did now. He was glad he had brought the chain. The winds on the mountain could be fierce. The chain would weigh him down—keep his body from being blown away, like a dried leaf.

He explored the large protected area. There were no trees, but he did find some brush and small plants, and even small pools of water.

There was a sudden shift of light, and he was momentarily blinded. The sun had moved from behind Pico, filling the area with sunlight. He rubbed his eyes. Everything was a soft blur.

A column of smoke rose from the crater beyond him. On occasion the islanders had witnessed a thin plume of smoke rising from Pico's summit. Emilio even remembered a time when the smoke had formed a distinct cross. People had photographed the sight, which became a famous postcard. Now he watched the smoke rise, then spiral down toward him, as if blown by a sudden gust of wind—although he felt no wind.

Gray flakes swirled and fell around him. He reached out his hand. Snow? Dry snow falling in sunlight?

The flakes danced around his head. Emilio smiled. No, not snow—butterflies. A cloud of a thousand gray butterflies. The man hadn't been lying after all. He reached into the satchel and brought out the net that the naturalist had given him. The butterflies flapped their silent wings. The sun shone all around now, and he could see that some of the butterflies were violet, some yellow, while others were streaked in red, green, and blue.

Emilio peered down the mountain, toward the distant villages where his family and friends went about their lives. But everything had gone gray, nothing was clear. Still, he wondered: Did they stop and look up, gazing at the mountain, wondering about old Emilio?

"Hey, you down there. I don't need to die with you. Up here, I have wings!" He laughed and jumped up and down. Gone was the pain.

A shadow moved across the sky, and he saw that the clouds had indeed come. The butterflies flew around him, encouraging him to join them in their flight. He grabbed hold of the chain. He wrapped one end around his right leg.

Death belongs down there, he thought, not up here where strange butterflies dance around a smoking volcano, as if coming from the earth itself. He swung the net, but they flew right through it. So many, that some kept falling to the ground, in layer after layer. Just like snow.

The Blind Man of Praia Negra

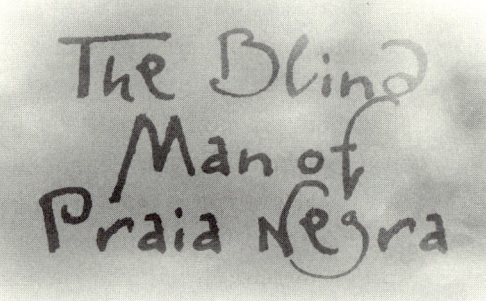

IN THE VILLAGE OF PRAIA NEGRA, THE BLIND MAN, TIMOTEO, PAINTED a furious sea with seven thousand white flashing teeth, in a frenzy, against the background of a black, hungry night. The teeth shattered and fell helplessly upon the black rocks of the islands and the sleek black sea. The looming shadow of Pico rose darker than the dark of the night, as if threatening to consume all, and the moon glowered blood-red in a sky that extinguished all traces of light from the stars.

All of Timoteo's paintings were night scenes.

He had worked frantically against the ever-quickening onset of his blindness, and though no one could explain how or why, he still managed to paint, despite the fact that he could no longer see the colors of his paints, or the canvas, or the faces that accompanied the voices of those who spoke to him.

He ordered that all his colors be mixed very carefully, according to a detailed list of careful measurements he had made himself, with the precision and expertise of a chemist.

Everyone in Praia Negra remembered when Timoteo first discovered he was losing his eyesight. He suddenly proclaimed he would become a painter. Every day for many months he was seen with paper or canvas and a palette of paints, dabbing a bit of yellow with red or blue, a touch of green with a streak of brown or red, but mostly black with blue or purple, or the deepest, bloodiest violet.

"What is he doing?" Ermina Gonçalves asked. "What is he painting?"

"Nothing," said her friend and neighbor, Maria Lourdes. "Look, it is only a big splash of paint. That's all. He's blind. How could he possibly paint anything? Everyone knows the man can't even see."

The villagers exchanged knowing glances. They felt sorry for the old man. It was a pitiful sight.

Timoteo laughed away his doubters and skeptics. "They think it is funny to see an old blind man like me paint, do they?" he said to those who came to look, or to no one at all; for though he could hear voices, he saw shadows at most. "Why should it be so strange to paint what I see, here"—he tapped his head—"why do I need eyes for what I already know, what I have already seen a thousand times?"

"First, I must learn to feel the colors, how to mix the shades. All the secrets of light and shadow." He would go back and cover the piece of canvas with black paint, and then lightly streak the black with a thin glaze of blue or green.

After nearly a year had passed, he was completely blind. Now he finally began to paint things, places, actual pictures. The villagers flocked in disbelief to see for themselves as Timoteo painted the familiar landscapes of the sea and the islands, the boats, and of course Pico towering majestically to the heavens.

"Ah, *meu Deus*!" Rui Manuel de Andrade shouted. "Come look here!"

Timoteo's neighbors stood gaping at a scene that was too foreign, too inexplicable, and too frightening to comprehend. Some turned away, quickly averting their eyes with a whispered cry to heaven. Others stood rooted, unable to move or speak, looking at a vision they should have recognized. After all, anyone could see it was Faial—indeed, Praia Negra—that Timoteo had painted. And yet there was something else there, something which, although all of them had felt, none of them had ever actually seen.

There was something suggestive that lurked, camouflaged in the painting. It was concealed in the blend of colors and brushstrokes, in the imagery of ocean and fields, of houses and nighttime skies.

"There is some trickery here," Maria Gomes cried out. "Some kind of devilry, no doubt."

It was as if the sea and land had swallowed the sun and all its radiant daylight. Night was everywhere—even the shadows appeared to cast shadows. More than that, although it was clearly a painting of a night scene, anyone could perceive that the night merely masked something else, something that pervaded the entire picture and all life on the island. It was this which all of those who looked upon the painting recognized, even without truly understanding it or being able to point it out, scratching their heads as they tried to see what could not be seen.

All seemed to mock and mimic the darkness underlying everything, even the glimmers here and there that weren't the night or its shadows: a luminous streak of violet that peered from the murky body of the ocean, an errant reflection cast by some careless fool passing by with a lamp, a scarlet tear from the nocturnal rumblings of the volcano, a streak of dull orange or brown that was the last gasp of a frail moon, squeezed and strangled by the calamity of oppressive night. It was as though the feeble light was life itself, laughing at the people because life wasn't theirs, because the night, the shadows, and their mortality were all they really possessed.

Everyone who peered at Timoteo's paintings felt strange internal stirrings, unnamable aches, longings for things that had never been or could never be.

It was the same with each and all of Timoteo's mysterious works of art. The villagers were increasingly frightened of the visions; soon only a handful of souls dared gaze at them, and then only fleetingly, as if fearful they might be caught looking at some forbidden and perhaps dangerous object.

"There is some evil here. After all, if a blind man cannot see, how then can he paint?" Gil Matos said.

"And why are they all of nighttime, darker than night?" asked Maria das Flores.

"Perhaps because he is blind and cannot see the devil is revealing himself by guiding Timoteo's hands," Hortênsia Pereira suggested.

"I told you all!" Gil Matos said. "Only the supernatural could be behind something like this."

They watched, suspicious and fearful, while Timoteo stood in the dark night, sniffing the air. "Ah, there is a full moon tonight." The villagers shuddered as they looked up to find the blind man was right. It suddenly seemed colder, too, which wasn't due to the moon or any chill in the air but to the fact that Timoteo somehow knew things he shouldn't have known. He uttered crazy, impossible things. "There is a young man down that street who is dreaming of a woman he loves on the very next street," or, "There is a young girl across the channel, over on Pico, who has just now discovered how terribly alone she is, and the unbearable secret fear she has that she will be seen for who she truly is, that the eyes of others will pierce though and peer into her frightened heart," or, "A whole village will soon awaken to the thoroughly sad and painful realization of the terrible price of beauty."

Still, Timoteo, unaffected by the disturbances he caused his neighbors, continued to paint, slowly, methodically. A lone boat on the water between Faial and Pico, with a tortured thread of light from an oil lamp in the boat's cabin allowing a sliver of silver to peer out from the inexorable shadow of darkened boat, sea, island, and nighttime sky.

After he had finished this latest painting, Timoteo put away his paints and supplies. "I have nothing more to do," he told the few villagers who bothered to listen. "I will paint again only when I have eyes with which to see." He sat alone in his room.

Life continued as it always had in and around the village of Praia Negra, and the people quickly forgot all about Senhor Timoteo, the sad, old blind man whose collection of paintings in the room in which he lived were his only source of illumination.

∼ ∼ ∼

Maria Antónia, the youngest daughter of Sonia and José Vasco dos Santos, had grown into a fine young woman, and carried the secret of the sea and the wind in the eternal ebb and flow, the waxing and waning, the bewitching gray-green gaze of her eyes. She came to Praia Negra from the village of Quebrado do Caminho, on Pico, to stay with her mother's sister's family, after her own mother had taken seriously ill and her father had disappeared. Her mother wasn't expected to live, so arrangements had been hastily made.

Maria Antónia's aunt took one look at her niece's eyes and made a prophesy: "Ah, there will surely be trouble here."

She was a girl who caused waves of disturbances wherever she went. Not by anything she said or did, but by her mere presence—her eyes, for one, her voice, her smile, and her overwhelming and all-encompassing beauty. No one could look at her without thinking that the old stories were true, that she was descended from a creature of the sea; that her mother's grandmother had washed up on the shores of the island, a mermaid, or siren, or one of the one hundred Nereides said to inhabit the ocean depths. She had decided to live among humans on dry land after falling in love with a young man of the island. And anyone who had any doubts on the matter simply had to look into Maria Antónia's eyes to see that it was all true, for every shade and hue of the ocean could be observed in her eyes, which seemed like two glass orbs in which the sea ebbed and flowed.

In the dark they gave off a luminescence that was startling to all who saw them. "My God," her uncle Fernando Gomes said, "It is as if she has the moon inside her."

Timoteo was Maria Antónia's great uncle on her mother's side, and he lived alone in the small one-room house next door to the girl's aunt. Maria Antónia was eager to see her Tio Timoteo, whom she hadn't seen since she was a little girl. But she was told that he couldn't be bothered, that he was old and needed to be left alone.

Day after day Timoteo sat in his room trying to summon the memories of things—people, clouds, shapes and colors, the lost faces of his family and friends—vague images that came and went, which slipped though his fingers like the finest sand.

Maria Antónia finally couldn't wait and snuck timidly up to the door of Timoteo's house and knocked. She was overjoyed to meet her uncle, even though she'd been warned that the old man could no longer see and was as helpless as any baby. Timoteo opened the door.

"Tio Timo"—her pet name for him—"it's me, Maria Antónia. Please, come with me, Tio!" Maria Antónia said.

"Alas, my dear," he said. "You have come for me at last." Maria Antónia pulled him away from his darkened room, determined to lighten her uncle's life.

For the first time in many long months, Timoteo laughed and came alive. Upon this meeting little Maria laughed away the clouds that had dimmed his sight. Taking him by the hand she led him on a walk through town.

The air in and around Praia Negra vibrated and hummed as Maria Antónia walked down the streets, to church or the market, to school, or to play with the few girls her own age.

Her effect on the town was registered by the scale of silent complaint that accompanied the countless sighs, the tender longings, the restless emotions and, of course, the glances that followed not only her every move, but also her expected arrivals, her painful departures, and the constant hopes of seeing her pass by.

In the cafés and taverns, on the streets and in the market, people stared, swept up in the daydreams caused by a glimpse of Maria Antónia.

Maria Antónia ordered Timoteo to stop all his nonsense and resume painting at once. "You can see as well as anyone, Tio Timo," she said. "I don't want to hear anything more about you being blind. Please, now, paint a picture for me." She sat by as he set up his paints and canvas once again, for how could he refuse this delightful child?

She possessed an otherworldly quality. Her rosy cheeks appeared as if they had been kissed by the angels, and her mouth promised undying love, joy, and laughter, the promise of an unquenchable life.

One of the villagers happened to pass by the spot where Timoteo stood painting; he stole a quick look, then stopped in his tracks, struck speechless. He finally managed to cry out. Others rushed to see. Soon a large group stood and gasped in disbelief at Timoteo's new canvas.

It showed the stone mosaic of Praia Negra's narrow main street, the shadowed gray of the buildings hugging each other closely, familiar to them all, but there, like a dream, a vision, almost completely obscured by the lightless night, were radiant orbs, two eyes that seemed, even there in the night, to represent a separate world unto themselves, a tiny glimpse of a heaven none of them could ever have imagined.

Timoteo found, much to his surprise and amazement, that his vision was now illuminated, the shadows dissipated, the fog cleared; images danced before his eyes, and he drank up everything there was to see.

People found it difficult to tear themselves away from the painting. They knew those eyes. They had seen them and felt them tug at their own hearts, felt the pain and ache that accompanied such a sight. All of them had tried to follow and fathom those crystalline pools—their radiance, their impenetrable mystery, their indefinable color—to discover the secret realm in which they resided and reigned.

But, everyone asked themselves, how did Timoteo, the old blind man—he who couldn't see anything—how was it he saw that which he painted, and painted so beautifully, how had he made them no less enchanting and powerful than the real ones?

"I don't need these to see," Timoteo answered impatiently, gesturing at his useless eyes. "I knew she was here the moment she arrived."

Day after day all of the townspeople—not only the men and the children—came by to gaze at Timoteo's pictures, at the radiant colors, as if seen for the first time, because no one could fully describe what those colors were.

"They are blue," one man said.

"No, they are green—green as the pastures of Pico," said another.

"You don't know what you are saying," said a woman who chanced by. "They are gray. Anyone can see that!"

But everyone knew they were all of those: sometimes blue, but with gray mostly, then streaked with green, always in combinations never seen before.

"Her eyes are so deep," said Paulo Carvalho, one of the girl's many admirers.

"As deep as the sea," said another.

"You mean the heavens," insisted Paulo.

It was truly a spectacle to behold. Here was a young woman not yet fully grown, and yet her effect upon everyone was such that, if she told them all to jump off a cliff into the sea, or swim to Pico, they would have done it without hesitation—though don't think for a moment that people actually said or did anything to show the girl that they thought the world of her. Their tongues and mouths were incapable of expression; even their hands and arms lost all sense in her presence, becoming useless appendages. They communicated instead with long faces, eyes staring off, sometimes a silly smile on the lips—flickering, fleeting, then gone—and with sigh after long, forlorn, breathless sigh.

Timoteo and Maria Antónia were now nearly inseparable. He hobbled after her, chasing his visions—which only remained his, some said, as long as she was near—or sat her down beside him to glean the deepest depths of the mysteries behind the shapes and colors he now saw.

Ah, how the neighbors began to talk!

"She should be sent back to her mother," Maria das Flores said.

"And Timoteo, too," said Hortênsia Pereira. "He should be sent away."

"Yes, we should be rid of them both!" said Maria Furtado.

"How can a blind man suddenly walk around like anyone else?" Gil Matos said.

"It's a sign of more troubles to come, just wait and see," Hortênsia said.

"No, certainly nothing good can come of this!" Maria das Flores agreed.

Timoteo laughed at their fears and their gossip. And he painted each of the townspeople, one after another, but in a manner that none had ever seen before.

Dona Lucia da Silveira, the wealthiest woman in the village, whom the others always called *a judia*—the Jew—paused beside Timoteo as he stood before one of his paintings, paintbrush in one hand and palette in the other.

"So, old man," she said. "What are you painting this time?"

"Only what I can see and nothing more," he replied. Others, too, stopped and looked, though none could identify the figure in the painting, familiar as it was, until Dona Lucia herself glanced at it and realized in an instant who it was. Herself, and no other! But not her as she'd been photographed once or twice in her youth. In this portrait she noted the shadows and secrets of her innermost heart, her deepest desires and her deepest fears, all exposed for the entire world to see!

She nearly fell in a dead faint.

The next day, Senhor Velas happened to pass by; he too saw himself upon one of Timoteo's canvases. He gasped and looked around quickly, wondering if any of the others had noticed. But no one said anything. Couldn't they see?

And so it went day in and day out. Each day a new inhabitant of the village appeared with the help of Timoteo's hand and brush. Each looked in horror, then reddened with embarrassment and quickly glanced round, certain that everyone else had seen, and was laughing at them.

All their faults, weaknesses, and vices were shown glaring, exaggerated, and grotesque under the painful illumination of Timoteo's artistry.

"There's been nothing but trouble since that girl arrived," the villagers remarked. People began to shun her; even her friends suddenly found reasons to stay clear of her. Maria Antónia's aunt didn't know what to do; she was afraid of the poor girl. "That girl and her family are cursed," the aunt said. "Why did I ever take her in?"

Finally, word came that other arrangements had been made. Maria Antónia was shipped back to Pico to stay with her grandmother and her brothers, in Santa Inês. The townspeople came and saw the girl off, waving, crying, telling her what a dear, beautiful child she was, how they loved her, nearly worshipped her, how sorely missed she'd be—forever in their hearts and memories.

After Maria Antónia left, the village let out a collective sigh.

Once again, Timoteo walked around in a cloud of despair, unable to see and at a complete loss around his paints. He couldn't even manage to hold a brush correctly anymore.

"My eyes have gone," he was heard to say. "My sight has left me."

His canvases stood empty and his paints dried out. Timoteo sat helpless, no longer venturing forth without the assistance of a friend or neighbor.

Until one day, when he left to go for a walk alone. Several villagers saw him wandering about, though no one realized that he was out by himself. He did not return, but it wasn't until the next day that people began asking what had happened to him.

"I saw him yesterday, walking out of town," someone from the next village said. The villagers searched everywhere but Timoteo was nowhere to be found.

He was never seen or heard from again. The three old sisters who lived down the road offered three differing hypotheses as to what had happened to their neighbor. Maria Aurora believed he had walked blindly into the water, headed toward Pico, and drowned somewhere between the two islands. Maria Anúncia said he had left the village for Horta or some other place where there lived a former sweetheart, who now cared for him. And Maria Clementina voiced the opinion that he had successfully traversed the strait between the islands, had found Maria Antónia, and could see perfectly well again with the aid of that girl with the bewitching eyes, whose side he thereafter refused to leave.

A Night on the Town

FOR A SHORT TIME AFTER HIS DEATH, GUILHERME GOMES CONTINUED to practice his unrivaled brew of bad habits. He was even more than usually morose, for the realization that he had not reached paradise came as a huge disappointment. Instead, he remained in the village of Santa Luzia, on the island of Pico, where he had lived the entire fifty-eight years of his life. Not only had his surroundings not changed, now that his life was over, but he also discovered that a hangover was just as unwelcome a thing, whether one was dead or alive.

When he finally stumbled into the house—drunk, as well as feeling somewhat the worse for being dead—his wife, Rosa, scolded him as if nothing had changed.

"You lousy good-for-nothing," she shouted, when she found him sneaking in through the back door. "Why don't you come home sober for once?"

He waved her away with his hand. "Please, not now. It's been a hell of a day."

But the next day was no different. He was gone in the morning and only crawled home in the afternoon after the bars had closed.

"Brute, drunk again, are you?" she confronted him. "Why did I marry such a man?"

"Why are you shouting?" he said, trying to dodge her words, which came at him with such unexpected force. He was surprised to find that not only her words, but her voice, too, had a very unpleasant effect upon him. It was yet one more disappointment for someone who had thought death would bring eternal peace.

"Just look at you," Rosa said, shaking her head.

"I'm not drunk."

"Not drunk. Am I blind? Where are you going now?"

"To find work. I'm going to make money."

"Hah! The only work you do is lifting a bottle to your mouth. You're as useless as those drinking pals of yours."

"Quiet, woman," he said. "Does the whole world have to hear?"

"Why not? Let them know how I have suffered. The whole world should know what you are!"

"What I am? What about you? You could drive a saint to drink."

"And you talk too much for a dead man!"

Guilherme roamed the house, trying to get away from his scolding wife, who wasn't about to let up on him simply because he was dead.

"Your poor mother suffered, and I, too, suffer. She warned me before I married you. There is no end to the suffering your family has brought into the world."

Guilherme ran away, running in death from the sharp-tongued woman, just as he had often run off when alive.

Some days later Rosa heard her husband had bumped into an old friend, who had informed Guilherme that since he was dead he should return to the cemetery. "That's your proper place and there you'll be able to avoid scenes with Rosa." Rosa, however, doubted Guilherme was capable of staying away since, if nothing else, he was a creature of habit.

Before going back to the cemetery, Guilherme returned to the house in an uproar, completely indignant. "I'm leaving!" he told Rosa. "I refuse to be hounded and tormented any longer."

"Fine, you simpleton. Go on and leave. No one else could put up with you. You'll see."

So Guilherme ended up doing the sensible thing at last—he went to his grave.

Meanwhile, Rosa struggled as she always had to take care of the children, to scratch enough food out of the patch of soil behind the house, to sew, to tend the animals, to cook and go to church.

It was difficult and the only blessing was that it had always been difficult; she had never had a glimpse, not even for a moment, of anything else.

It was lonely too, however, and after some months, though she wouldn't admit it, not even to herself, she decided that it was proper and necessary for her to pay a visit to the cemetery where her husband was buried.

"If I don't the whole world will be wagging their tongues about it," she said.

Rosa climbed the hill for the first time since the funeral and sat down on a stone beside the dry and cracked mound of earth that was Guilherme's grave.

"Don't think just because I'm here that I've come to sweet-talk you. If you had to go and die, at least you could have seen fit to leave your family in a better way. Little Maria Alice is sick again. Your son Vasco is as stupid as his grandfather and doesn't know from nothing."

During Rosa's outburst Guilherme remained glum and silent, listening to the stream of words with the stoic patience only the dead can truly appreciate.

"Yes, we're in fine shape," Rosa continued. "Our chickens are laying fewer eggs, and the cows—I won't even begin to tell you about the cows. It's a shame! It is only because you are a Gomes that my life is not fit for a dog. If I'd had any concern for the world I would have drowned your children and myself and wiped out the family name, and this curse, once and for all, instead of prolonging this agony. Then I wouldn't have to live a life of such misfortune."

She returned to the cemetery repeatedly to pour out her complaints, her problems, to vent her sorrows and anger to a husband who found, much to his dismay, that he could no longer run away. At the same time, however, Rosa always made sure to tend to the gravesite. She swept away dirt and leaves; she wiped the stone cross tenderly; she even brought flowers to place on the stone. And Guilherme smiled as best he could, for it had been many long years since Rosa had shown him such tenderness, and nobody had to tell him that, while honey is sweet, the bee stings.

One day while tidying up the grave, wiping away dirt and pulling out weeds, she saw a bone. When she bent down to examine it, she discovered that a whole pile of bones had emerged from the ground.

"So, you couldn't stay put, huh? I should have known. Don't tell me, you're on your way to some bar. Is that it? Well, we'll just see about that." Of course she couldn't know if that, indeed, was where he was heading, or if he had simply been pushed out because of overcrowding. Soil was precious on the island. Generally there were far more rocks than dirt. Because of this, people were frequently buried atop their ancestors.

Rosa left to find a large wicker basket. She returned to the cemetery and carefully placed each bone in the basket, which she carried home. Then, with the utmost exactitude, she set all the bones in an order that more or less resembled her husband on a simple bed she had made up for him on a mat on the floor. Most of the bones, if not precisely in the correct arrangement, at least were fairly close.

"There, now you can see for yourself what goes on around here," she said, "and I don't have to break my back climbing the hill just to visit you."

She tried to ignore the shame and disgust she felt, seeing him in such a debilitated condition. He looked even more frail and helpless than when he was alive.

"If I didn't know you so well, I'd think maybe I got the wrong husband by mistake. You look terrible."

She brought him an old broken mirror.

"Take a look at yourself."

It was true. Nobody could deny that Guilherme was looking his worst.

The poor man, stretched out helplessly, suffered a daily deluge of insults, drowning in the ceaseless flood of her fury. He wished he could live again, if only to leave the island, to swim if he had to, and find some remote corner of the world where he would never again have to endure the harsh sound of his wife's laments and condemnations.

He cursed the shifting in the earth that had caused his bones to break free.

"Why couldn't I have been pushed down deeper into the ground instead of into her arms?" he asked the interminable silence.

Rosa paraded their daughter past Guilherme.

"Look. Look at this poor child, sick with everything imaginable. Tell me who will take her for a wife?"

Guilherme tried to turn over but remained immovable.

"Here's your son," Rosa said. "Another one of fine Gomes stock. He'll grow up to be a drunk just like his father and his grandfather. Thank God you're dead and can't knock me up again."

It was at this time that Guilherme became aware of a different thirst than any he had ever known, a profound and tireless thirst that gnawed at his existence like the most unbearable longing, a thirst not even death could kill.

If only I could drink, he reflected, at least a sip or two of wine, perhaps I could endure this. But of course he was in no condition to drink, unable to move, trapped as he was in the world of the living and no longer in the ground, the very ground which appeared to have leached out his last bit of strength. He wasn't even able to drink the moisture of the earth through his parched bones, which he might have done had he still been in his grave.

He dreamed of his friends holding court in the bars, drinking and joking among themselves, so far removed from their homes and their problems, while he was imprisoned with this woman who refused to leave him in peace.

What is the point of dying? he wondered. If one only continues to suffer?

During a rare moment of stillness in the house, he noticed a strange sound that reminded him of coins falling, of water rushing down a stream, of birds chirping. Then he heard voices speaking. It was his daughter and several of her friends, come to poke fun at him: this poor man, naked and helpless for all the world to see. At least Rosa could have had the respect to cover him up.

The girls finished with their fun and scampered away, leaving him alone and sulking. But in a short time half the town decided to pay a visit to Guilherme's home. Everybody wanted to take a peek at the remains of "that no-good husband of Rosa's." They crowded into the room, laughing and poking at his bones. One or two spilled some wine on him, which—though he cursed their carelessness—his parched bones relished nonetheless.

Rosa even allowed that buffoon, Francisco, who ran the market, to bring his dog into the house. The dog began licking one of Guilherme's leg bones and nearly ran off with it before somebody finally had the decency to chase the dog away.

The townspeople, greatly amused at his expense, were oblivious, of course, to the terrible insults Guilherme unleashed upon each and every one of them: "*You*, Maria *azelha*—the dimwit" and "*You*, Marco *o lobo*—the wolf" and "*You*, Alfredo *frouxo*—the weak."

Finally they left. Rosa seemed to be in a good humor for once. She walked from room to room, whistling and singing, picking up after her neighbors.

Guilherme wished he had something particularly vile to say to her, but he was silent in his rage.

He was awakened later that night by a warm breath, smelling of *aguardente*. He was being carried.

"*Shh!*" he heard, as several people clumsily removed his bones from the house. There were three or four, he thought, all evidently drunk.

Outside they whispered to one another, and Guilherme recognized his friends.

"Let's take him to Pedro's first." It was Manuel.

"That was always his favorite hangout." He recognized José's voice, too.

"Come on, let's hurry while the night's still young." Roberto, of course! Where there was José, there was Roberto.

The whole gang was there, ready to drink the night away. And they had gone out of their way to include their old friend, Guilherme, for a night on the town, just like old times.

He felt like weeping, but just then Roberto tripped and dropped the handful of bones he was carrying. He kneeled, scrambling to pick them up, and no one except Guilherme noticed that one or two were left behind in the dirt.

They reached Pedro's café and seated themselves around one of the tables. They ordered drinks and laughed.

"What will Rosa do when she wakes up?" Manuel said.

"She'll know. If there's a drink to be found, Guilherme will stop at nothing!" José said, laughing and pounding the table. "Only Rosa could drive a man away even after he's dead!"

"What are you devils up to now?" Pedro asked.

"Here," Roberto said. "Look who we brought along."

Pedro stared down at the bones the others had piled on one of the chairs.

"It's Guilherme!" the three drinking buddies proclaimed.

"Now I've seen everything," Pedro said. "You fools are crazy."

They ordered more drinks, and every once in a while Manuel took Guilherme's drink and poured a little into the dead man's grinning skull.

"Still drinks like a fish, doesn't he?" Manuel said.

Guilherme floated in a sea of happiness, as he silently blessed each dear friend who poured a drink onto his bones. But it really wasn't the drink that set his old heart aglow, as much as it was the sweet companionship of friends, friends who not only understood him but appreciated him as well. This, he now discovered, was what he had longed for all these many years.

After another round of drinks they stumbled out into the night and made for Vergilio's place, accompanied by several of Pedro's customers. When they got to Vergilio's, Guilherme was distressed to find that more of his bones had been lost along the way.

His friends began recounting the tragicomical stories of Guilherme's life: how he could out-drink anybody; how he sponged food off friends and neighbors whenever Rosa kicked him out of the house, sometimes for weeks at a time—a tale that brought tears to all the listeners' eyes. They enumerated the many times Rosa had made public Guilherme's frequent sins, how she always said she was through with him and wouldn't take him back and how, time after time, once her anger wore off, there Guilherme would be, back home again. "Even after he died, she still took him back!" Roberto said, to a thunderous applause. They also told how if Guilherme knew of somebody worse off even than himself, he would fetch that person a bottle, and hand over his last scrap of food; how he never had a cruel thing to say about anyone. Even when drunk he was everyone's friend and no one's enemy, unlike Luís Carvalho, who picked a fight with somebody every time he drank. All this brought cheers and calls of what a worthy friend Guilherme had been.

They hadn't been too long at Vergilio's before one of the men decided they should go elsewhere; after all, this was a night for celebration. It wasn't every night that they could drink with a dead man. They must be sure to make it a night to surpass all others, a night that would be talked about for years and years. A night to reestablish Guilherme Gomes as the master of serious drinkers once and for all!

Through the night Guilherme was transported along the old familiar roads, past the homes of his friends and relatives, past the places and people he had known all his life. He heard the songs of his buddies and the voice of Father Fagundes offering communion, he saw his wedding and his newborn children, and during all of this he felt an integral part of everything around him, as if all the moments of his life were occurring simultaneously.

They staggered from place to place, carrying Guilherme's drenched bones each time, pouring drink after drink down their friend's open mouth. They stumbled and crawled onward, and whenever they dropped the ever-lighter stack of bones, they picked up as many as they could find, and continued on to the next place.

Guilherme didn't know if it was the drink or the fact that there was now less of him, but he was feeling the effects of the rowdy night. Everything seemed more and more distant, sights blurred and sounds grew muffled and thin, until they became a pleasant hum in the air.

Still, Guilherme felt he was where he belonged: he was with good friends, in the village where he had been born. I'm at home, he thought, and he had never been happier in all his life. His friends were celebrating him as a hero, as if he had somehow become greater with his death. Guilherme wondered if they could see, as he now clearly saw, how the aura of death transformed everything, much in the same way that the drink had always done, making him feel, in a way, greater, grander, part of something far larger than himself. If it were possible he would have beamed with a wide happy smile of joy.

His friends grabbed whoever was around to join them. Some decided to start over and headed back to Pedro's Café; others trailed off to home and sleep. Some found themselves holding a bone, without remembering exactly why or how they had come into possession of it, and so tossed it in someone's yard, or along the side of the road.

Soon only Manuel, José, and Roberto remained, along with a scrawny dog, which had followed them around for the past few hours. The dog sat under the table and gnawed on a bone.

"What a night," Manuel said, slurring his words.

"I never drank so much in all my days," said José.

"We should go home and rest," Roberto said.

The others agreed. The skies had lightened. It was close to dawn.

"Say, where is Guilherme?" Manuel asked.

They looked around, but Guilherme was gone. They quickly searched the ground and their pockets. Nothing.

"Wait." Roberto pulled out a slender bone from his coat pocket.

"That's it? All that remains of our friend?"

"What will Rosa do?" José said. "Everyone knows that woman's a powder keg."

They quickly returned to Guilherme's house, placed the single bone on the ground, then made like the wind for their own beds.

The next morning the news spread across the town, whispered from ear to ear, making its way inside all the open doors and windows.

Manuel, José, and Roberto were back at Pedro's by then, silently nursing the effects of the long night. There they heard the story of how, in the middle of the night, Guilherme Gomes had somehow managed to run away, how even in death he was completely irresponsible, how Rosa had woke in the morning to find several of his bones left behind in the yard in his obvious rush to clear out of town.

The three men looked up at the grinning skull, perched upon a high shelf behind the bar. Pedro had found it while cleaning, early in the morning. They raised their glasses in one more salute to their old friend, who appeared much happier here, in his new resting place.

The Wounds

THE WOMAN SAT IN HER BED, PROPPED UP BY HUGE HEAPS OF HEAVY pillows. Blankets lay scattered every which way. She looked, to her husband, like a large, plucked bird tangled in a messy nest.

"What's that horrible smell?" her husband said.

"What smell?"

"That smell. Like . . . I don't know what."

"I have no idea what you are talking about," the woman said, as she returned to the careful examination of her wounds.

The husband threw his hands up in disgust and turned away. He had developed a method of refusing to see what he did not wish to see. His wife, on the other hand, did not live outside of her fascination for the wounds, which for months now had broken out and spread upon her body. They had appeared one day and had stayed with her ever since. From the very first she could not leave them alone. Her husband awoke at night and found the woman bent over, poking the sores with inquisitive fingers, lifting them to her nose and sniffing at them suspiciously.

"What do you hope to find there?" he asked.

She merely huffed, or shook her head, or ignored him and remained silent, as though to speak was beneath the dignity of the fate she suffered.

The husband tried his best to avoid these unpleasant spots. It was inevitable that he should brush up against them, or forgetting, reach to touch his wife, who would scream, cringing at his touch, not from any pain she suffered but because she felt that her wounds were hers and hers alone. For the longest time he was only permitted the barest, most fleeting of contacts. And then not even that. In any event, they were horrible to look upon.

The husband suspected that his wife was causing the wounds to worsen, enlarging them with her constant attention.

"Where will this end?" he asked. "Why do you do this to yourself?"

The woman burst into tears, crying without a break for an entire day and night. Now she began to complain of the accompanying pain, whereas until then the wounds had been painless. Night after night she howled, and her screams invaded the nearby streets, filling the empty silence.

Advice flooded in from the neighborhood: pray, bathe twice a day in the natural baths at Veradouro, spread the infected areas with the pulped bodies of banana slugs, boil this root, take these herbs, burn these leaves. Meanwhile, her husband spent more hours in the cafés and elsewhere.

"I don't have a wife anymore," he commented sadly. "I have an open wound chained to her holy bed of agonies."

His friends drank with him in solace.

"What's wrong with her?" he asked. "Why does she carry on so?"

The others could give no answer, except those few who were inclined to agree that God in his wisdom had chosen her as a martyr.

"It's a mystery," they said with a shrug.

He went home to find her lying on the bed, moaning, and looking at her various wounds with a handheld mirror. The house was in terrible shape, and the children wandered half-clothed and filthy. Everything was falling apart.

Her body was swollen with the extravagances of her wounds, which bloomed like malignant, evil-smelling flowers. Her husband fretted, worried about her increasing size. She now took up the whole bed, as if it were all just another attempt to outdo him, to—by sheer bulk—force him out.

"Look at this place!" he shouted. "Do we all have to rot? Must we suffer too? Are you just going to sit there while we starve and the house comes falling down around us?"

"It's your fault!" she shrieked. "You did this to me!"

He stormed out of the house and walked down the street toward the café. "I did this, she says. I did what?" He wondered if this could be the result of her having children. But then other women had children. This didn't happen to them. "She sits there day after day hurting herself in this way, unable to do anything else, ignoring me, the children. And she blames me! What will come of us?"

The café was bustling. He ordered a drink and stood at the counter. He didn't feel like sitting with anyone, or talking.

I feel this terrible weight, he thought. Right here. He thumbed his chest.

∼∼∼

He returned home late, determined to finally do something about the intolerable situation he was in.

"It's a reflection of our lives," his wife stated.

"What are you talking about?" The smell was overpowering, and he held his nose shut.

"My wounds. They are a symbol of our life."

"Enough! If anything they are a mirror of your blackened soul."

She burst into tears.

"That's it!" he shouted. "I've had enough." He gathered the children and some belongings and left to go stay with his sister and his brother-in-law, Oliveiros, on the other side of the town.

His wife's ceaseless cries were heard all that night by everyone in the entire town. The next day several women went to visit her, to see if there was anything they could do.

The woman's husband, now peacefully lodged at his sister Emilina's home, heard repeated reports about his wife's condition.

"They say she hasn't stopped crying," Emilina said.

"Well, at least she's done shrieking for now."

"And that her room is filling with all the tears she's shed."

"What do I care? Let her weep. She has caused enough misery for us all to have a good cry."

"Poor woman!" he heard everyone whisper. "How she suffers. And alone and so very wretched." Anyone who endured such misery was worthy of respect.

The women of the village came and prepared food for her, as well as every known concoction of herbs, ointments, and salves, in an attempt to relieve her suffering.

The pain was without respite. Her wounds continued to worsen.

"Your wife is dying," Emilina informed her gloomy brother, who had been bored to silence by the repetition of his wife's name and ailments.

"We are all dying."

He went to work at his menial post in one of the countless government offices, where he performed his tasks with the usual steady, lackluster pace. His sister had her hands full with his as well as her own children. Meanwhile people who'd heard rumors of the stricken woman came from all over to see for themselves the miracle of her pain and suffering. They brought their ill, their injured, their blind and needy.

"They say your wife's wounds are now pouring forth a river of black blood," his sister said.

"Serves her right."

"Shouldn't you be with her?" Emilina said, wondering why she had allowed him to stay.

"What can I do? She doesn't want my help. She only wants to suffer. No one can even share that with her. She's a very selfish woman, that one, hoarding her precious agonies."

"There must be something you can do."

"What? I couldn't plug up all her wounds for her. There are more of them than there is of her."

"They're saying she's a saint."

"Yes, and I'm Judas. It's only because she's so stubborn and greedy, too, that they are suggesting she is worthy of being considered a saint."

"What do you mean?"

"She could do nothing else. She needs her wounds, as much as a hermit needs to be alone to forget life, or a drunk needs to drink. She's not making any sacrifice but pigheadedly doing precisely what she wants to do and what she can't help but do."

With that he stomped out of the house and went to wash away his woes with drink.

Several weeks later, after they had dragged the poor unfortunate Father Alves to have a look at her and say a few words to Christ and the Virgin Mother on behalf of the ailing woman, and after exhausting every possible remedy, even those guaranteed by the great-granddaughter of the last *benzedeira* of Água Zangada, who was rumored to be a sorceress of unequaled powers, the woman finally gave up and expired.

Still, her husband didn't believe it. "It's a trick," he said. "What next? She is faking, can't you fools see?"

They tried to convince him to go have a look for himself, but he couldn't be persuaded.

"No, I refuse to go over there. Soon she'll grow tired of this pretending to be dead—you'll see."

"But senhor," they said. "She doesn't move, or speak."

"So what? Anyone can do that."

"But her heart doesn't beat."

"I admit, she's very crafty, that woman. I know. Look how long we were married. Very crafty."

His sister, exasperated by her brother and his children, who seemed destined to stay forever in her house, came to tell him the news. "She is dead. I saw for myself."

"Don't believe it. She's made fools of all of you."

It was some time before he finally gave in. The townspeople told him that proof of the miracle lay in the fact that, here, weeks after she had died, there was still no odor of a rotting corpse; it was as if she were only asleep, like her husband had said all along.

He decided at last to go have a look for himself.

He walked into his own home and barely recognized it. It was spotless. There were candles burning everywhere, and the hush of many people milling in and out of the place, who were nevertheless subject to the solemnity of their purposeful visit.

"Looks like a chapel," the husband cried. "Where's my wife?" He was led into the bedroom. Everywhere, new furniture had replaced the old. Even the huge broken-down bed, which his wife had converted into her own private universe, had been replaced with a much grander, modern bed.

He gave a whistle.

The people—mostly strangers, though there were some he knew—continued to file past the woman, to whom he now turned his gaze for the first time in months.

What they said about her was true. She sat like a giant stone Buddha, her enormous belly and her legs and arms swollen like tree trunks and all covered with crater-like sores. She hadn't decomposed at all, but was perfectly intact, as though she slept.

Many of the visitors mouthed prayers and genuflected, while almost every one of them left money on the plate at the foot of the bed.

He waved his hand in front of her face. Her blank eyes didn't flinch, but stared out as though seeing something extremely far in the distance.

The procession urged him to move forward. "Go on," he heard, "Let us get close to her. Give us a chance to see."

He suddenly snapped to attention. "Get out," he shouted.

There were grumbles of dissatisfied voices.

"Go on. Viewing hours are ended. Come back tomorrow morning." He shuffled everyone out of the house, and went back to his sister's.

He knew he couldn't stay forever at his sister's house; it was too small for both families, and besides, her husband Oliveiro was a *conservador,* always spouting off about his right-wing politics. He needed his own house back.

In the morning he returned home with his children, who assisted in taking money from the strangers for entrance and selling lottery tickets. In the evenings, the husband closed down the house and went to sleep beside his wife, happy, even content with his life, dreaming dreams and smiling the smile of a happily married man.

The Lost Voice

CELESTINO AZEVEDO HAD NEVER STOPPED TO THINK ABOUT HIS OWN voice. He always took it for granted, unless he strained it, or became sick and found it faltering. But he never thought he might lose it the way someone might lose a hat or a walking stick.

Until that very day, when Celestino's voice chose to abandon him, he had never given it a second thought. He assumed he'd come down with a sudden illness that would pass in a day or two. After several failed attempts to speak, he decided not to talk for the rest of that day and night, assuming that time and rest would provide the remedy to cure his speechlessness. It was less difficult than he thought it would be, for if someone spoke to him he nodded, smiled, or winked, to which they ascribed their own meanings, and continued talking as though he were participating in the conversation.

After twenty-four hours had passed, however, Celestino opened his mouth—but again nothing came out. Not so much as a moan or a gasp. Not a sound.

The same thing occurred the following day.

After three days he thought about seeing a doctor in the city, but people in the village have a saying: "You go to the doctor when you're ready to die." Since Celestino was in no way ready for death, he put off going to the doctor. Instead, he waited, anxious to see if his voice would return. After all, who ever heard of such a thing? One day you're going along fine, and the next you cannot speak. He'd known of people who went blind, but never a healthy man losing his voice for no apparent reason.

As he lay in bed searching even in sleep for his missing voice, his mouth opened, as if to groan or grunt, but only silence would greet him.

In the night itself he heard sounds: faint whispers and rustlings. The meanings of these late-night susurrations eluded him; they sounded like the murmurs of the sea rather than the wind or a human voice, though Celestino sensed something human in them, some desire or longing which had increased in intensity to the point of becoming audible.

His friends and neighbors repeatedly asked what was wrong. "Are you sick? How come you don't speak?" By signs and writing he made clear that he could not speak. They were quick to think he was having fun with them. "Come on, stop pulling our leg, Celestino, you're having a nice joke, eh?"

At first people reacted to his inability to speak by raising their voices, as if by hearing their shouting, he would suddenly be able to respond.

Some took his silence as an affront. "You always thought you were better than us, and so now you refuse to even speak?"

"I've lost my voice," he wrote on a notepad, showing it to each and every one he met. Those who felt insulted continued to feel insulted and stormed off in a huff, muttering to themselves about people who could stand to be taken down a peg or two. Or else they would repeat what they had said, as if he hadn't heard them.

Others began greeting him with a slap on the back, "So, did you find your voice yet?" "Are you still in your vow of silence?" some joked.

But his voice still showed no sign of returning.

Sometimes he saw the butcher or the refuse collector and they would speak in serious tones: "Say, I heard your voice last night, over by the graveyard." Or, "I could have sworn I heard you shouting in the middle of the night down the Avenida da Liberdade, where that irresistible vision of loveliness Maria Almeida lives."

Celestino didn't know if they were merely jesting, or if, as the old saying goes, every big lie contains a small truth. So he went to the places where they told him they had heard his voice. He couldn't say that he heard it himself, but thought he could feel an echo of his voice lingering in these places, the way you can taste a smell or smell a taste. Maybe it was only the fact that he had been to all of these locations a thousand times over the years, and had likely spoken on numerous occasions in each one, so that something of his voice remained.

He left his house and roamed the streets, hoping to take his voice by surprise. But how does one trap a voice which can be heard here one minute and over there the next, which can speak in a shout or a whisper, and fall silent at will?

One night, as Celestino was searching for his missing voice, he ran into Carlos Monteiro, the shoemaker. Carlos called to him, and seemed in a particularly good mood.

"Celestino, you old devil," Carlos said, nudging him with his elbow.

Celestino looked puzzled. He shrugged, and made a face to show he didn't understand.

Carlos grinned. "I heard you speaking at the window of the widow Dona Amélia. I never knew you could talk like that. Why, you're a poet, Dom Celestino. A real Don Juan."

"But I haven't gone by Dona Amélia's house," Celestino wrote as fast as he could on his notepad.

"I heard you with my own ears."

"I can't yet talk," Celestina wrote.

"It was your voice, I'd swear to that. And the things you said to her. Why, you had Dona Amélia giggling, and crying, 'Stop Celestino, please stop!' I wish I could talk like that. A tongue of honey."

Celestino walked away, scratching his head. So now he was Dona Amélia's lover! What next? The trouble a voice can cause, he thought. Usually one has control over what one says. This circumstance was new to him and showed just how dangerous an unguarded voice could be. He realized he had no idea what his voice was capable of saying, what words might serve its purpose, which was as deep a mystery to Celestino as the mystery of a woman's heart, or the sea, or the secrets of the stars.

What can I do? Celestino wondered.

Meanwhile he caught wind of his voice's latest mishap: it had caused a row at the Taberna Rui Gomes, uttering some derogatory words into the ears of Fernando Lima, the sausage-maker, about a local fisherman named Manuel Gomes, and then mouthing a challenging response in Manuel's ear.

The *taberna* was tiny, a few square feet, but was soon filled with fists, shouts, and oaths.

Celestino wandered, keeping to himself for fear of hearing any more frightful news. He had to find a way out of his troubles before things worsened.

He thought about Maria Teresa, a schoolteacher he had always admired but had never spoken to, though he had wanted to for many years. She was a woman of unfathomable calmness. She'd never married, though men certainly did notice her. She had quietly rebuffed each of them, as though she were waiting for a particular suitor who was scheduled to come and marry her at an appointed hour.

Celestino had watched Maria Teresa from afar, marveling at her calmness, and her impenetrable smile, which always seemed to say, "I know he will be here, if not now then sooner or later."

Somehow he had never found his voice around Maria Teresa. There were always reasons why he couldn't speak to her: "She looks busy. I'll talk to her later. It's the wrong day, nothing good ever comes on a Friday. There're too many people about, I'll wait until she's alone. She's alone, it'll make her nervous. I'll wait until there's someone else around."

How ironic, he thought, that his voice was now running loose, speaking as freely as the worst gossip. Why hadn't it gone to speak at Maria Teresa's window instead of Dona Amélia's?

Before he knew it, Celestino found himself sitting outside Maria Teresa's house, taking stock of the situation. The problem, he thought, is far too complex for any doctor to solve. He was on the verge of going to the police with the demand that they assist him in capturing his rogue voice, when he remembered Maria Ginete Toledo, the *feiticeira* who was said to be descended from Gypsies or Spanish Jews, and who was renowned for her mystical abilities.

The door to Maria Teresa's house opened and closed. A moment later she stood before him.

"Good afternoon, Celestino," Maria Teresa said, the ghost of a smile on her lips.

He stood speechless, wringing his hands. He could only nod and take out his pencil to write something.

"You don't need to write, Celestino. I know what has happened," she said, her voice rich and deep. "I will help you to find your voice, and then perhaps we shall talk, you and I?" He stared at her face, in which he read an assured strength and determination. He could only nod dumbly. "This has gone on long enough," she said.

Maria Teresa walked with slow, measured steps in the direction of the plaza at the center of the village.

Celestino wondered at the miracle that had just occurred. He hadn't said a word. Instead, Maria Teresa had spoken, and had spoken to him about the two of them. "We shall talk," she had said.

The two of them continued on toward Maria Ginete Toledo's house.

Celestino stumbled down the street like a drunken man, until they stopped at a small stone hut by the rocks of the shore, where Maria Ginete Toledo lived.

"Go on," Maria Teresa said, pointing to the door. "I'll wait here."

Celestino stepped forward. Tentatively, he knocked at her door. Please don't take offense, he thought. Don't change me into a toad or a lizard. He didn't know what to expect from Maria Ginete. Being a *feiticeira*, she was capable of anything.

The door opened and he came face to face with Maria Ginete Toledo, who exclaimed, "What took you so long?"

She didn't wait for him to reply, but boldly took hold of his arm and led him inside. "I've been expecting you," she said.

She sat him down at the table where an oil lamp cast a dim glow to the room.

"Why didn't you come sooner? Wasting time trying to find your voice, like a man chasing his shadow. Didn't you know you needed help? Of course not, you're a man! Need I say more?"

Celestino gave no reply other than a shrug. Maria Ginete spoke forcefully. Her eyes pierced him; she could see in his soul. She was a roundish, plump woman, old, but strong as any man. She wore a black dress, and a shawl; her hands, arms, and ears were draped with gold.

"Come, sit down," Maria Ginete Toledo said, indicating a chair beside her table on which sat a black cloth, an oil lamp, and a smoky glass orb.

She sat herself down at the other end of the table, then asked to see his hand, which she grasped with what felt like a claw, studying his palm with a discerning eye.

"Hmm, just as I thought," she said.

Then she peered into the glass. Celestino stared too but could see nothing. The glass looked as dark as the cloth on which it stood.

Maria Ginete mumbled a few incomprehensible words and grinned.

"Yes," she said, nodding, and releasing Celestino's hand at last. "Go home, and then wait."

She stood and shooed him out of the house without ceremony.

"What about my voice," he managed to write before she slammed the door behind him.

"Your voice will be found, but not by you. Go home and wait. That is all."

The door closed behind him, and Celestino stood alone in the night. He felt utterly without hope. If Maria Ginete Toledo could not help him retrieve his voice what more could he do?

He looked around but Maria Teresa was nowhere to be seen. Where had she gone? And why had she left? It was odd that she hadn't entered Maria Ginete's home, too. She *had* been there, hadn't she?

Celestino shook his head. He followed Maria Ginete's advice, not out of any hope that remained, but because he could think of nowhere else to go.

As he walked home he again heard those sounds like muffled murmurs. They mingled with the wind, the occasional barking of a dog, the crowing of a rooster, and the lowing of a cow, growing louder with every step. As he passed Maria Teresa's house the sound grew to such a pitch that he had to stop his ears. It was a song of desire unlike any he had ever heard before, a wail of passion, a surge that threatened to consume everything.

Then Maria Teresa was there, walking up the street as if to meet him. He smiled, thinking that he could recognize her from a kilometer's distance.

Celestino stood frozen on the stone street, his mind filled with the sound of unleashed longing. He watched her approach, until he realized that the sound was coming from him.

His mouth was open wide; he was shouting her name at the top of his lungs.

A moment later she was in his arms.

"Celestino," she gasped. He clung to her, and couldn't stop saying her name, over and over. She led him inside, shushing him calmly and quietly, as he let all the words that he had saved over the many years, all the things he had longed to tell her, finally have their voice.

Constança's War with the Elements

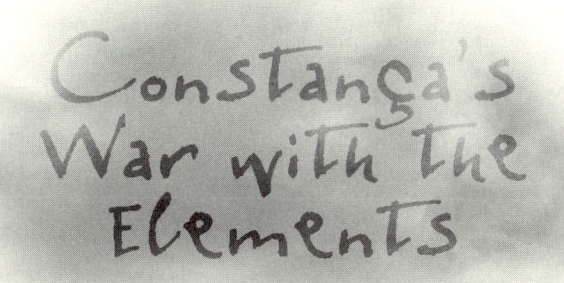

AS THE FIRST TREMORS SHOOK THE EARTH, CONSTANÇA MORAIS OPENED her eyes and rose from her bed for the first time in seven years. She scurried to the back door and called to her children, though her voice sounded like the rasp of an old gate that had rusted shut. It was soon discovered that the tremor had opened a vent in the ground out in the fields. Steam and smoke emanated from the crack, and the smell of sulfur filled the air.

Constança's husband, Álvaro, was instantly cured of his love for the grocer Pereira's wife. Even though Constança had been asleep for seven years, she knew everything that had gone on.

"In my dreams," she confided to her best friend, Filipa, "I heard and saw everything."

Without Constança saying a word, Álvaro felt the heavy weight of shame and remorse for the accumulation of all his terrible sins over the last seven years, illuminated—or so it seemed to him—by Constança's sudden wakefulness, and doubly illuminated—he saw the sins, like a shopping list—whenever he looked upon the unforgiving eyes of his newly wakened wife.

He resolved at long last to reform himself. "How could I do this to the woman I love?" he was heard to ask. "Still, what right has a woman to sleep for seven long years?"

It was a question no one was prepared to answer.

Constança felt her insides twist up in knots with the knowledge that her daughter, Manuela, was no longer living her own life, but had somehow slipped into Constança's misbegotten youth. It was as clear as holy water the mistakes she would soon make. So she ordered Manuela to make her way to the church on her knees, every day of the week, to do penance for improper behavior with a neighbor boy whom Constança had never liked, and whom she banished forever from her sight, from the property, and from Manuela's heart.

"How could she see that Gonçalves boy?" Constança moaned. "He is just as bad as his father and everyone else in that family of bad blood! One drop of their blood is enough to cause ruin for seven generations!"

"Are you sure?" Filipa asked. "I never saw them together."

"Of course, I'm sure," Constança declared. "I've seen the way they make eyes at one another. I must put a stop to it right now. Trust me, once you start down that road, I know all too well where it leads."

Their son, Francisco, who had hired on with men who were making a new road and repairing an old one, was gone much of the time working. And when he wasn't working he drank and chased women.

"I should think," Constança said to Filipa, "that something, perhaps, in all that time would have changed, but look, nothing is different. Nothing ever changes."

"Perhaps, you shouldn't be too hard on them," Filipa said. "After all, there was no one around to make sure they didn't go bad. Manuela is a beautiful girl; it's not her fault that Carlos Gonçalves finds her attractive."

"I too was cursed that way, and look where it got me," Constança replied. "No, this suffering will do her good. She will be strengthened for it."

Álvaro was asked how it had been, living with a sleeping woman for seven years.

"You get used to anything," he said.

The men snickered and laughed because all of them knew that Álvaro had had no shortage of company during those seven long years of sleep, and because they knew that now his time of plenty had come to an end.

"She was always foremost on my mind," he said.

"Why did it happen?" Filipa asked Constança.

"I do not know. Perhaps to see things clearer."

"And Álvaro?"

"Look what a good husband he has suddenly become. He was never like this. Not even before we were married."

It was true. Álvaro now waited on the woman hand and foot. Not only did he stay away from other women completely, but Constança was all he could talk about.

Constança sat in her bed—from which she claimed she could not rise—holding a copy of her favorite book, *The Unsolvable Enigma*, by Sebastião Augusto do Canto e Castro. She could not remember when or even if she had read it, though she knew its contents from beginning to end, in that mysterious way she seemed to know everything. "Ah, Filipa, how that man could write. A regular philosopher!"

"I have no time for books," Filipa said. "Why fill your head with all that nonsense?"

The villagers ran out of their homes at the occasional rumblings of the earth, and the sounds of the buildings shaking. They set up blankets outside or, if they were lucky, a tent, where they could sleep beneath the glass eye of the moon. Constança, however, ignored the tremors and refused to budge.

"What is this thing for?" Constança said with disgust, spreading her hands at the bed on which she lay. Filipa, who sat nearby, looked up.

"What?"

"This bed. I have no idea. I haven't been able to sleep since I woke."

"I knew this would happen!" said Álvaro, who had just come up to the bedroom door to ask if Constança needed anything. "You used up all your sleep during those seven years."

"You mean?" said Filipa.

"She will be awake for seven more years."

If the previous seven years had been difficult, Álvaro found this new condition even worse. He slinked through the house at all hours like a thief, shying away from the ever-open eyes of his sleepless wife.

Sometimes she seemed to stare without seeing anything, then she would appear to look right through him. "I can't hide," Álvaro said in desperation. "Her eyes are everywhere." It was more than he could stand. Still, he knew this, like her long sleep, was just one more sign that his wife was attempting to escape her fate.

He thought of running off to see Pereira's wife, but he knew if he did Constança would be there, watching. It was utterly hopeless.

"Where can a man go when, no matter where he goes, there are those eyes seeing everything?"

Álvaro stepped outside. He watched Manuela making her way to the church, taking each painful step on her bare knees, as she now did every day. There were tears running down her cheeks, but the girl suffered the punishment imposed by her ever-vigilant mother in silence, clutching her rosary, ignoring the cuts and bruises.

Constança watched Manuela from her window. "She will thank me later for this. When she stops living my life and finds her own."

Filipa propped Constança as comfortably as she could, where she could look out from the bedroom window, and watch life pass by like a stream. Sparks of commentary fired from her mouth, her lips opened with a burst, then closed, tightly drawn together like the strings of a purse. She took notice of everything that passed by her window.

"Maria Aurora is in love," she said, looking after the figure of her neighbor.

"What have you heard?" Filipa asked.

"Nothing," Constança replied. "I don't need somebody to tell me something when I can see with my own eyes Maria Aurora walks as only a woman in love can walk."

She continued to gaze down at the quiet dirt street.

"There is nothing down that road," she said. "It is empty."

"What are you saying, Constança?" Filipa asked.

"Look around you. Nothing is as it should be. When did this happen? Was it always this way?"

Filipa didn't understand a word of Constança's wild talk and, frightened that some new turn of events had taken place, ran off to find Álvaro.

Meanwhile, Manuela had returned from her visit to the church. She sat in the back of the house, quietly knitting a shroud out of spider webs and the translucent wings of insects. She had forgotten to speak since her mother had awakened. Nor had she looked at anything or anyone. She had worn a path between the house and the church, and not once had she wavered from that track.

Now she was blind, deaf, dumb, and invisible—though she still heard, spoke, saw, and was seen in her own fashion.

Álvaro, tired of feeling the penetrating gaze of his wife, and anxious from feeling exposed and unable to hide, came home. "I will never set foot outside this house again," he said. "I can't go out there. Not like this!"

Álvaro sat back in his chair, content to relinquish the life of coming and going.

He watched Manuela, no longer recognizing her as his own daughter, as she toyed with beams of light in the corner, sending them like tamed birds to fly this way and that. She spoke in cheerful tones to the voices of the air, sea, and earth, which sang their songs in a manner that had nothing to do with time or birth or death, but only with that which had always been, and would be forever. All Álvaro saw was her mouth opening and closing, until she was done with her shroud, and then he saw nothing.

Had his daughter vanished into thin air, or had she taken flight with a pair of luminous wings?

Constança's gaze, like a *milhafre*'s, saw even beyond the bend of the road and the buildings that obscured the view. The shaking of the earth had gotten worse, and as everyone seemed to breathe the fear that Pico would erupt, they constantly looked over to watch the mountain.

"The whole world is upside down," Constança said, while Filipa prayed hard and fast for the speedy recovery of her dear friend and companion. "Maria da Conceição," Constança continued, "is very unhappy with her lot and, in fact, I see that she is in love with Pedro's oldest boy, Eduardo, who of course went off and married that hussy, Maria Matos."

Constança went on and on, listing who should be with whom, and what so and so should be doing with his or her life.

"You!" she shouted when Guilherme Gomes, drunk as usual, tried to sneak past unseen. "You should go off and hang yourself. Your poor wife and children! You are good for nothing."

And when Senhora Velas walked by, "You, senhora, are living a lie!" And then when Senhor Campos paid a visit next door. "Senhor Campos, you married someone else's wife!"

Manuela once beautiful and now invisible, hid her good looks with the disguises of her friends, the elements. They took her laughter and happiness, her smiles and pretty features, and the natural radiance of her spirit. Those things that had once been hers now soared in the air with the feathers and songs of birds, swam with the fish, and blew with the winds; they moved silently in the sunless subterranean pools of water, coursed through the soil to smile upon the trees and plants, to kiss the green grass and fruit growing in such rich abundance; they became mixed with the rains which fell down upon everything.

Manuela left the house dressed in a hundred *never minds*, a thousand *nos* and *nays*, the words and sentiments of her prayers. In the shadow of her fasting and resolve and renunciation, she traveled the course to the church on her knees, which no longer registered pain. She felt instead only the voluptuous pleasures of her knees torn raw by the rocks, the stones and dirt embedded deeply in her flesh.

No one looked at her. No one saw.

Except Constança, who breathed a sigh of relief. "She has saved herself, that girl. If she keeps this up she will become a saint!"

Manuela carried a growing bundle of spider-web refuse, of dirt and sticks and leaves, while at the same time shedding the husks and skins, the remains of her vegetable, mineral, and animal body.

Filipa told Constança that she had heard Senhor Campos was leaving for America. "They say his wife will wait and join him later," Filipa said.

"No," Constança said.

"No?"

"This land is the land of mother's milk. He will go and no matter how far he goes or for how long, he will think of this island, and all it means, wringing his heart. How he was born here, how all he knows is here, and how far away he is. He will not be here, and he won't be there, but lost somewhere between. Until one day, when he envisions the island and his return, the future home he will have with Maria, when he will slip and fall into the sea and drown with the fishes. Even then he will swim toward here, but he will not reach our island. And she, she will sit in her window and look down the road for the rest of her life, unable to leave, wondering if and when her man will return, along a road from which nothing will ever come."

Carlos Gonçalves, the boy Constança had discovered was in love with Manuela, tried to lose himself in his work, feeding the cows, milking the cows, leading those very cows out to the fields every morning, tending to the grapes which grew in his yard. But he kept hearing Manuela's voice in the trees. He heard her sweet whisper as birds flew overhead; he saw her face reflected in the pools of water and lakes. Her laughter could be heard when the wind rumbled like a waterfall of stones down the side of Pico, and her sparkling tears filled the skies at night; even the rain tasted of Manuela. He felt her forbidden flesh on the ground under his feet. He bent down and kissed the earth, kissing the likeness of Manuela, which he found impossible to resist.

∼ ∼ ∼

At the end of seven long and arduous years, Constança finally closed her eyes and slept. Álvaro and his wife had grown old, but Manuela was even older.

She now took care of her parents, though her beauty had been transformed into the earth and into those things that sprang from the earth.

The earth seemed to sleep too, the shaking and rumblings having momentarily subsided.

Manuela's brother Francisco found a young schoolteacher for a wife, and she moved into the house after they were married.

Manuela married her virtue and solitude, her stony silence and prayers, her eyes of blind wood, her deaf ears of interminable patience. She clung to the whitewashed rock of her arms and legs, as well as the various nests, webs, and assorted odds and ends she stitched together, and found herself giving birth to two large and silent twins of misfortune. Her children were also mute, deaf, blind, and invisible, as lifeless as Manuela, only more so, since they were nothing more than the husks and skins of her misery that over time she had discarded, shedding like a snake.

Carlos, the boy who had loved her, had become hardened to the endless work. He had grown into a man and, instead of loving Manuela—the woman he hadn't seen since Constança had banished him from her home—he loved the fleeting images of her in the air, earth, water, and plants.

He drank deeply of the kisses of Manuela, in the red wine that came from his vines, in the grapes which grew of Manuela, of the earth that was Manuela, of the water, the air—everything that was Manuela.

Álvaro crept off one night, dragging Constança down to the cemetery. "We don't need to hang around here anymore," he said, though his words fell on deaf ears. He stood by the tiny piece of earth where all their ancestors had been placed, one after the other. "This is our place."

He planted Constança on top of the bones of the other relatives. Then he crawled in himself and covered them both with a heavy blanket of fertile soil. He listened to the slow language of the centuries, of fathers and sons, mothers and daughters, brothers and sisters, aunts and uncles, and so on. He listened to the incomprehensible words of the eons, to the wordless messages that spoke the phrases of endless repetitions: of the ebb and flow, of the blind tenacity of life, pushing ever forward, striving to continue. The incredibly slow descent of the one, intermingling with the impossibly slow ascent of the others, until they were all one: one father and son, mother and daughter, brother and sister. Even Constança and Álvaro became one, melding with the mountain from whence they had sprung.

Manuela swept up the dust and dirt, the dry husks and spider-web sheddings of her twins, and brought them together to the church, where they sat by her side as she prayed. Fortified by drink, and drunk with the overpowering love he felt for the Manuela he found in everything, Carlos didn't even see her when he passed the three of them on their way to church. Whenever he came near her, clouds quickly gathered all about Manuela's body and the spiders, whose shroud masked her beauty, worked at a fantastic pace, spinning new webs to cover her face and shield her eyes from the boy she was forbidden to see.

Constança/Álvaro worked out the secrets of the universe. They and the ancestors who were part of them had been absorbed into the bowels of the volcano, the spring water under the ground, and the vegetable life of the island. Of course, part of them lived on in the form of Manuela, and no one had forgotten that, either.

Least of all Álvaro/Constança.

By this time Francisco and his wife had several children of their own. Naturally they took over all the rooms of the house to contain their growing family. Even so Francisco soon began to think that the house was too small for all of them. "Why shouldn't I sell the land?" he asked. "With the money we could move to America, like Senhor Campos."

"Yes, we could have a big house there, and pretty things for us and our children," his wife said.

They had forgotten all about Manuela. No one had seen or heard her, so there was no reason to take her into consideration.

Francisco tried to find someone interested in the land, in the house and cows. Somebody suggested Carlos.

He began to think perhaps he could convince Carlos to take over; after all, he had enough money. Then Francisco and his wife could make plans for America, where he could get a better job.

Constança/Álvaro's voice cried out at this scheme. The hitherto silent stones began to speak: "After all the work I did, what will happen to Manuela? Especially if that boy moves into our house. I won't have it!"

"They can't sell the house!" Álvaro/Constança added.

"Or move to America!" said Constança/Álvaro.

"Our blood, spit, and sweat is in this soil. How can they sell it and leave?"

The one who was in fact many asked themselves an endless list of questions, and grew even more furious at the lack of answers.

They shook the ground with their fury. Constança/Álvaro was determined to keep Manuela away from Carlos, Álvaro/Constança was just as adamant about not losing the house, and both were equally determined not to have the family move to America.

"I'll rip a hole in the ground to swallow that Carlos boy."

"And I'll move the earth and knock the house to the ground—so they've nothing to sell."

Their anger shook the island. Constança/Álvaro did try to swallow up Carlos, but only succeeded in destroying Carlos's house. Álvaro/Constança's anger bubbled up at a weak spot in the earth's surface, just off the shore of the island.

Lava boiled the ocean, and bellows of steam and smoke shot high into the air. Ashes rained down on everything. The sea turned red from the fires.

Francisco and his wife threw themselves on the ground and cried. "How can we stay here?" she said. "Nothing is safe here."

"But now our land will be worthless."

The ocean was covered with a layer of fire, bubbling and boiling; thunder rocked the world from the air, and Pico shook from deep within. The night turned blacker than black. There were no stars or moon at night, and no sun during the day.

"We must go before we are killed," Francisco's wife cried.

Pico roared and rumbled as the whole island shook.

They gathered what little they could carry and fled, leaving everything to Carlos for next to nothing.

Manuela whispered to the crack in the earth behind her house. She tried to soothe the fires and calm the noisy earth.

Carlos and some others ran to the shore, prayers flying out of their mouths. Many brought food and gifts to appease their angry God. All of them made many promises to reform, to better themselves, repay old debts, give more to charity, stop bad habits, do good turns. "Please, anything you ask, dear Lord, if only this terror will stop."

Someone carried the silver crown of the Holy Ghost, its dove with outstretched wings atop, in a show of penitence and prayer. Another brought out a brightly painted statue of Our Lady of Miracles, who smiled with supreme beneficence upon the devastation.

"We will honor you with a procession of thanks every year, if you stop this," they promised. Here and there men and women alike fell to their knees moaning, weeping, and crying for help to a litany of saints. Novenas were offered—nine weeks of prayers to Our Lady of Sorrows, nine special offerings to Saint Isabel of Portugal.

Several idiot children and adults of diminished capacities came out to help, guiding people this way and that, going where they were needed. Old women ran from their homes, shrieking and pulling at their hair. Grown men cowered on the ground.

Manuela tried to find her twins, but they had disappeared. She kicked the earth and pleaded for her innocent babies to be given up. The earth responded—thanks to Constança/Álvaro—by trying to take her instead. She heard her mother calling, "Manuela, Manuela, come now my child, forget everything else. Come with us."

Manuela fought back, but Constança/Álvaro was cunning and powerful; she destroyed many of Manuela's trees, as well as her animals, lakes, and pools, the fields of grass and even the thin layer of fertile soil that had captured Manuela's most precious gift; for Constança/Álvaro was of the hot inner earth, of the lava that seeped from the living core whence the lineage of all life sprang. And frankly there was more of her—her and all the ancestors past—than there was of Manuela, whose hold was rather tenuous.

Someone shouted, pointing up at the sky, "Look, there, a face!" There were clouds above Pico, and indeed they did form what was clearly a face—with eyes, nose and mouth—though only Carlos recognized the face as Manuela's.

The battle between Manuela and her mother waged on while everyone else was busy saving those who could be saved, as well as attempting to placate Álvaro/Constança, who ripped a gigantic gash on the ocean floor, churning the sea and filling the sky with black clouds and explosions.

Then the heavens exploded with a burst of thunder and the rains fell, while lightning lit up the skies.

The argumentative voices rose in collective shrieks and bellows. Thunder shook the island from above, the volcano shook the island from below, and lightning danced between them both, as the battle became one between the earth and sky.

Fierce winds swept across both the sea and the island, sending waves crashing across the land and lashing everything with pelting rain.

∼ ∼ ∼

After twenty-nine days of continuous rain, Filipa slammed the door behind her and stepped out into the deluge. She had remained solitary after Constança had gone, but she was not going to spend the rest of forever locked up, afraid of a little rain. "God is displeased," said her neighbor Dona Maria Campos, who sat facing out her window, as if searching for something lost in that wall of water—perhaps awaiting the return of her husband, who was still searching for wealth in America.

"This is the end," Dona Maria said. "Soon we will all be swept out to sea."

Filipa mumbled. "If it does, well then, fine!"

"It's a wonder it didn't happen a long time ago. We should all be punished. Perhaps at the bottom of the sea we could be washed clean of the sins of this life."

"This rain can't last," Filipa said. "The skies have to dry up sometime."

She shuffled down the flooded street, her head and shoulders bent over by the furious rain. She passed the normally dry creek bed. It was overflowing.

"There has never been a rain such as this," the voice of Dona Maria followed her. "The tears of heaven are falling, for there is only sadness in this world."

"Even God cannot cry forever," Filipa said.

Filipa navigated down the flooded streets toward the bakery. The wind whipped around her and the rain found its way through her protective clothing and shoes.

The bakery was closed.

She headed for the market. Perhaps there would be a little food there. People had to eat.

Everywhere there was the sound of water: waves crashed against the rocks, water rushed down the streets, and the continuous rain fell everywhere, running off rooftops.

She looked out toward the sea and sky, but they were one. She couldn't tell where the horizon was or whether she stood at the bottom of the ocean or at the roof of the sky.

It was like Dona Maria had said—the end had come, and the only thing that continued was the misery of life, which knew no end.

Filipa knew right then what she had to do, and so she waded down the rivers which had once been streets, to go talk sense to that friend of hers, the only one who could end this nonsense, Constança.

The battle between the earth and sky had come to a ridiculous stalemate. The earthquakes and volcano had shaken many people and buildings into a state of fragmented and confused disarray; then the rains had destroyed much of what was left. And finally the winds had torn off roofs and uprooted trees, knocked down walls and cleared planted fields of any vestige of life.

In the wake of the storm there remained only dead animals, ruined homes, and those poor souls who had lost everything. Boats had sailed away with no one aboard to steer or guide the way, confusing the bottom of the sea with some safe distant port. Much of the island lay in tatters.

Hardly anyone remembered the volcano now. The earth's grumbling still frightened some, but most people were too numb to care. They had lost too much.

Filipa talked to Constança, imploring her to sleep and spare everyone, the poor living, those who had no such luxuries as rest and sleep.

"You've made your point," Filipa said. "Now why don't you let things get back to normal?"

∼ ∼ ∼

Constança/Álvaro saw it was no use: either they would have to destroy the entire island and everyone on it, or let Manuela go. Now that she had been stripped of her clouds, her spiders and spider webs, everything else—the trees, rivers, lakes, and gravel—had given the girl back her unequaled beauty. She was no longer invisible and Carlos, of course, was one of the first to see. He cried with joy, and she did as well, for in her time of invisible blindness she hadn't seen him at all.

They marched with the others to the edge of the island, offering a thousand good things if the volcano ceased its convulsions.

Now that Francisco and his family had left, Álvaro/Constança decided it was better that Carlos and Manuela have their house and land, to raise their own family. It was clear that the island would suffer a terrible drought and famine in the next year. Manuela would need someone at her side to help, in order for her and the farm to survive.

The island settled down and was quiet again. Though not before Constança/Álvaro managed to open the earth below Filipa's feet—where she stood talking Constança's ear off—in order to keep them company in the ground below.

Manuela and Carlos were soon married. The villagers slowly rebuilt their homes and stores, and replanted their fields. Álvaro/Constança worked hard to seep life back into the ground, exhaling their smoky breath from Pico's crest, and providing fertile soil for Carlos and Manuela's farmland. Even the part that was only Constança smiled, for there was now a spark of life in Manuela's belly. True, it was part of Carlos, but perhaps he wasn't quite so bad as Constança had once thought, and, in any case, it included part of her, too.

The Exile

FERNANDO NORONHA GRAPPLED WITH THE BOX THAT HAD ARRIVED with the morning mail and brought it into the house. The mailman made some comment, but Fernando's English was not good, and he was too excited and impatient to try to decipher what the man had said. "Yes, yes," Fernando said, waving the man away and closing the door quickly behind him.

He carried the box into the kitchen as if it were a precious treasure and carefully set it on the table. There was a springiness and joy to his movements that had long been absent. It *is* a treasure, he thought. He sniffed the box in delight, able to smell, even through the cardboard, the paper wrappings and tape, the scent of home.

"At last," he said, trembling with excitement. *A box full of Azorean soil*. Sent all the way from the islands, so many months in transit, and such a large, heavy box, too. And safe, not opened or damaged by careless handlers, not mislaid or lost as he had expected and feared might be the case. Not even seized by customs or postal officials, which he had also feared—although he wasn't sure why they would. Perhaps, the Azoreans would resent anyone taking any of their precious soil, their homeland, to some other land. And perhaps American officials would object to allowing the soil of the Azores, or any other place, to come into the country.

Fernando went to a drawer and took out a kitchen knife. He cut through the string that crisscrossed the box, then the tape and paper. He opened the flaps of the package, and sifted through the soil with his fingers. He smelled the rich, fertile soil of Faial—the same luxurious earth that many of the ancient Azorean captains had carried with them when they had sailed round the world, assuring that if they were to die on a foreign shore, they would at least have the comfort of being buried with the soil of their homeland.

"While it's true I am exiled from my islands," he said, "here, now, I have reclaimed a small piece of the Azores." This then was the true meaning of *saudade*, not merely to long for what is gone, what has been wrenched away, but also to feel that part of you remains there, in essence to be separated from oneself.

It was impossible for Fernando to avoid reflecting on what he had left behind. He often found himself peering from a window or doorway, expecting to see a neighbor or friend: the faces of people who knew and respected his family name, and whom he knew as well. Furthermore, the natural beauty of the islands also was imprinted in his mind, as were the unavoidable comparisons with what now surrounded him.

Here in California he had no friends; instead, there were countless strangers, streams of people seemingly without end—people who cared nothing for what was dear to him. Instead of the sublime majesty of Pico towering above the clouds, there were indistinguishable rolling hills and endless flat farmlands. Instead of the lush greenery of the islands, the fields here were yellow and brown. Instead of soil that was dark and in which anything would grow, in which it was impossible to quench life, he saw only the poor dirt surrounding San José, which, by comparison, was dry and barren. He saw endless vistas of dust and sand. It was a desert really. Not paradise, as he had heard. Instead of the cool ocean breezes, the air was hot and stifling, as if it sprang from the land itself.

He sniffed the box of soil again, then carried it outside, eager to pour it into a section of the yard, perhaps to cultivate a tiny square patch of life in this impoverished place, where the whole land seemed to cry out for all it lacked.

He found a suitable spot in the corner of the yard, where he had foolishly attempted to grow a few herbs—and in vain, as nothing but weeds had come up. He scraped away three or four inches of California topsoil, then spread the dirt from the box evenly over the ground. He tipped the package upside down, shaking out every last grain, then took the wrappings from the box to the trash can, burying them under the garbage so that his wife, Maria Isabel, wouldn't find them. The postage had cost him a fortune. He had paid his old friend, Rui Fagundes, to send the package and asked him to keep it secret. If his wife discovered the facts, there would certainly be a dreadful scene.

He sat back in a lawn chair and looked at the dark patch of soil. Already he could detect a slight yet distinct change in the yard. He closed his eyes. Yes, a perceptible, though subtle, change in the atmosphere, as though an errant breeze had blown across his islands, then carried the scent and taste of the Azores here, to give life to the dry, hot monotony of San José. He could feel it caress his face, blow gently against the hairs on his arms.

He closed his eyes. Is it possible, he wondered, for a person to be in two places at the same time, to be both here and there? It was the only explanation: his body was trapped here, while his heart and soul were where they had always been—on the islands from which they could never be severed.

His reverie was shattered by the sound of the children rushing home from school. José, Luís, Maria Antónia, and Maria Lourdes burst into the yard and surrounded their father, who remained in his chair, staring fondly at his displaced bit of homeland.

"Why aren't you at work, father?" Maria Antónia asked. She spoke Portuguese, though she and the other children were learning English very rapidly. Their father, however, had been unable to grasp the complexities of that language. It left a bad taste in his mouth; he thought the sound of English was harsh and vulgar, unlike Portuguese, which was a sweet song.

He patted his daughter's head as if to dispel her silly question.

"Yes," the others said. "Why are you home?"

"They decided to let me out early today, that's all." It wasn't true, but he couldn't tell them he had lost yet another job. At the same time, he wouldn't be able to keep it from them for long. Maria Isabel would have to know and, as in the past, would be very upset.

"Run along," he told the children. "Go off and play."

They left Fernando alone, ruminating upon the adaptability of children, who could be happy no matter where they were.

Maria Isabel came home late that evening. They spoke after the children had gone to bed. "You have to find a job you can keep," she said. "We need money for food, for rent."

"I cannot keep a job where I am not needed," he told her. Where they only gave you work for which there was no need, due to a vague obligation to his family name.

"Then find another."

"Work isn't easy to find," he said. "Jobs seem to evaporate here just like water."

"Do not joke. What about the bills?"

"I'll find something tomorrow."

Later that evening, lying in bed, he was aroused by the sound of waves breaking. He heard an eerie cry and woke his wife.

"Isabel, Isabel, wake up."

"What?"

"Do you hear that?"

"Hear what?"

"A *cagarra*. A *cagarra* in the yard."

"Go back to sleep. You were dreaming. There are no such birds here."

He was certain he had heard one of those strange creatures, whose cry was so human-like that the superstitious believed it to be a fateful portent.

Fernando smiled as he drifted back to sleep. Only in a place as peaceful and quiet as the Azores could you hear the ocean's roar, or the cries of birds which some believed were the souls of children who had died by drowning. Such stillness and silence didn't exist in this place of traffic and noise.

He shuffled through the days, searching for someone who owned a business and who was Portuguese, someone who would remember and say: "Ah, yes, this is Senhor Noronha, a good man." Not a man who should go around begging for a job, who should do menial work, who should get paid next to nothing.

He returned home each afternoon, seeking refuge in his garden, where the Azorean soil had seeped into the ordinary dirt of the backyard, transforming it, bringing a volcanic propensity for life. Such dirt contained both history and memory, it was where dreams took root and flourished.

He watered his patch of Azorean soil and sat staring at it, for what seemed like several minutes. But, when he finally rose, several hours had passed.

There was shade here, cool winds and the scent of familiar flowers.

One day he came home to find another box, this one sent by Jorge Ribeiro, a writer who lived on Pico. It was a very small box this time. He opened it cautiously and found it contained a shell.

Fernando, smiling like a saint, took the shell and set it on the patch of soil.

Maria Isabel arrived home in a sour mood. "We need money," she reminded him. "You must find a job, Fernando! What will we eat?"

"I am looking," he said. "What do you want me to do? Nobody wants to pay me to work." He had tried working as a gardener and in a factory, jobs for which he had no experience, no training. It was hard enough to find such a job. But then to find one that paid a decent wage, one that you could keep, that was another matter altogether. Because he couldn't speak proper English, he had to find work among the Portuguese, but there were many Portuguese who wouldn't hire him because of his family name. Unlike them, he hadn't spent his entire life working with his hands. His family had once been wealthy aristocrats, but that had been a long time ago, at the turn of the century, before the revolution that had toppled the monarchy. Things had changed since then. Though he was willing to do almost anything, his family history had set him apart. In the eyes of those to whom he appealed for work, nothing had changed. They couldn't imagine an aristocrat doing menial work. And they themselves were squeamish about hiring him.

"Anyone else would have found a job by now," Maria Isabel said. "Anyone else wouldn't give up."

"I *will* find something," he said, hoping the next day would bring a miracle, but knowing that miracles were few in this land.

That night he listened to the Azorean winds blowing across the garden, rattling the glass in the windows, moaning dark secrets in their ever-melancholy voices.

The next morning he approached the radio stations, hoping to find one he could interest in a Portuguese radio program, as he and Isabel had done several years earlier. Shortly after arriving in California, they had aired their own Portuguese show in San Leandro. They'd written the scripts and acted the parts, using their children, friends, and neighbors as actors too.

In addition to appearing on the radio, the family had put on plays and musical shows at Portuguese halls and high schools up and down the San Joaquin Valley: Los Banos, Modesto, Hayward, Merced, Gustine, Turlock. At the same time, they had written articles and poetry for Portuguese newspapers. Later they had moved their show to another station, in San José. But in time that station had shut down.

"It's too bad we don't have the money to start our own radio station," he'd said to Maria Isabel.

"Radio?" she'd said. "We are still paying debts and you want to have a radio station?"

"Our shows were very popular," he explained to the men who owned the stations where he applied for work. "We wrote scripts that were interesting, funny—people laughed.

"We also reported on what was happening back home on the islands, about all the changes Salazar's government said were finally being made. At last, we thought, things were improving for the people—until we went back and saw for ourselves that nothing had been done. It was all lies.

"We had been lied to, and had unwittingly helped to spread those lies through the newspapers and radio. No schools were being built, no hospitals. Life in the islands was just as difficult as it had always been. So we came back and printed the truth. We showed the people that nothing had changed, and since then we cannot go back. *Personae non gratae*.

"Our competition ran their silly programs, and didn't like us," he confided, reminiscing. "They said terrible things about us, so we returned the favor. More people began listening just to hear our fights.

"But after some time business fell. The radio station closed."

The station managers shook their heads. "We're sorry," they said. "We have nothing to offer you." They held out empty hands. There was nothing they or anyone else could do.

Fernando drifted listlessly through the town, wishing for another job, wishing to escape, wishing to see his home, to leave this country that seemed to turn people into beggars: please give me a job, please pay me enough to support my family, please let me keep my job, my future.

He occasionally stopped at a café to read the Portuguese newspaper, or to sit and think, while he sipped his coffee. The day would slip by quickly, leaving him with little time to search for work. It wasn't that he didn't try—it was just that a person could only try so hard.

In the Azores of old there would have been no such trouble. He'd had friends all over, and the government saw to it that he had a position in one of their countless offices. There was no money, of course. The family had lost its wealth when his father was still a young man. The manor house that the family had owned, and in which he had been born, was nothing more than a distant memory. It had been sold and turned into an orphanage. Even with his government job, and Maria Isabel's ability to make do with little or nothing, there was certainly not enough on which to raise four children. Then a bad business venture—he and Isabel had tried to start their own newspaper—left them with debts to pay. That was why they had come to America at the end of the war. Here, they thought, their children would have a chance for a better life.

But this country had nothing to offer him. What did America want with his paintings, his Portuguese poetry? What did America care about his noble family? Here he was just a nobody, like millions of other nobodies.

Jobs came and went, and Fernando found it was possible to work yourself to death in this country without ever having anything to show for it.

A few weeks later, there was another addition to his Azorean garden: a piece of basalt, sent by Laurinda Pacheco, a schoolteacher from Faial. Fernando wasted no time finding the perfect place to set the volcanic rock. With each new item, the garden grew more comfortable; there was a scent of life now, too, where before there had been only the arid heat.

He sought a temporary escape in his proliferating garden, attempting to shut out the cares and problems that threatened to engulf him.

The Azorean soil inched farther across the yard, expanding and regenerating itself, spreading bit by bit to cover the lifeless California dust. He smelled the fresh sea air, felt the wind and the veil of humidity of his island. He drank glasses of Azorean liqueur and apologized again and again for leaving the isles.

"How deep has the dirt gone?" he wondered. Perhaps the volcanic soil grew and spread deep down into the earth. If only he could dig down far enough and reach the Azores himself.

If he didn't know better, he'd have suspected that Maria Isabel—and perhaps even some of his neighbors—had mailed more boxes of dirt from the Azores to fill the yard. The idea amused him. Isabel would say that dirt was dirt, no matter where it was from. But of course there were worlds of difference. The proof was in what was taking place right here in their own yard.

He thought of his children. They watched American movies and listened to the radio, able to decipher that incomprehensible language. They longed to be Americans. Perhaps it was a good thing after all. But to forget Portuguese? To forget the Azores, and their name? To forget who they were?

When he wasn't out looking for work, Fernando eased the pain of his exile by setting up his paints and canvas out in the yard and painting scenes from the islands: the stone streets and whitewashed houses, the view from his youngest daughter's bedroom window in São Roque, the green fields of Pico and the sea.

In the mornings, from the dreamy vantage point of his flowering garden, he sat where he could occasionally see Pico in the distance, breaking through its shroud of clouds. And in the evenings, after sunset, he walked through the yard, smoking his pipe, recapturing it all, the way he had once drifted through the park along the Avenida da Conceição. He breathed the fragrant smell of flowers, sweeping aside vines and thick-leafed branches, as he recalled the familiar pleasures of Azorean life.

Maria Isabel was relieved when Fernando finally announced that he had obtained a job as janitor at one of the radio stations. His family was more than thankful, for to them it was a godsend. But to him it was one more cruel twist of fate, painfully reminding him of what his family had once possessed; he was reduced to cleaning up after others at a radio station, as opposed to having a radio program of his own.

Fernando swallowed his pride and performed the work he was assigned. It was one thing for the people from the islands who had known only poverty their whole lives, he thought. He too was poor, but he kept his dignity and did not forget who he was. They couldn't take that away from him.

His cousin had been president of Portugal before Salazar seized control of the country; his ancestors included kings, queens, and captains who had carried the Portuguese flag to Morocco and India, Africa and Brazil.

Even now, whenever people recognized his name, he would recount for them stories about these famous ancestors, sighing, listing their illustrious accomplishments over and over as if, by repeating them, he might somehow restore the family's position.

Sometimes, while he mopped the floor or polished a counter at the radio station, he would pause, lost in some distant remembrance. Though he often stopped to chat with whoever happened to drop by, he did his job with his jaw set in fierce determination. Nobody was going to say that he was too proud or too stubborn, that he thought himself too grand, or that he was unable to work like everyone else. Maria Isabel and Fernando withdrew from one another, each retreating into a profound silence. She was different from him. She was tough and would let nothing and no one hold her back. Isabel found work easily, gave piano lessons, could speak English and French. She would make do, whatever the resources, or the lack of them. She had that natural ability to create something out of nothing. And while she had less and less to do with him, she seemed to prefer her work to almost anything else.

She resented what she saw as her husband's lack of industry, his inability to better provide for his family. He wasn't like her grandfathers, whom she adored and whose memory she constantly invoked. One had left his island, on an American whaling ship at the age of seventeen, and had become a farmer in California; the other had started a successful business on the island of Pico.

She accused Fernando of being a dreamer. "You must make yourself useful," Isabel said.

She had summed up the problem. He was of no use in this time and this place. He should have been born a century or two earlier.

"I do what I can," he answered. Was it his fault if he wasn't like the common men and women who toiled endlessly in their daily lives? Could they write poetry and plays, could they paint or play the violin, or discuss the finer points of literature?

"What have you been doing anyway," she said, "but sitting in the yard and staring at the dirt as if you hadn't a care in the world?"

"Staring," he mumbled. "You've noticed the changes, too?"

"Changes? What changes?" Isabel said. "What are you talking about?"

"The garden."

"Are you crazy? What garden? Who has time to plant a garden?"

She hadn't noticed the new soil, then. She couldn't see the wondrous transformation that he watched day after day.

Fernando swallowed his pride and went back to work, sweeping and scrubbing, bending beneath the growing weight of indignity and disillusion in order to clothe and feed his family. But at the end of the day he returned home, holding his head high.

"I will not allow the world to crush me," he said to himself, looking forward to escaping into the sanctity of the garden.

His old friend, Rui Fagundes, had sent another box—not nearly as large as the first one, it was true, but still welcome. Fernando poured out the soil of home, further enlarging his garden.

The garden had become an oasis, providing shelter from the harsh heat of San José—the heat that dried up dreams, that baked love out of existence and vanquished one's hopes.

Maria Isabel came home and informed him that she was going to rent an apartment near San Francisco. She had been working at a new job there, shuttling back and forth for several weeks. Now she had decided to go there, with the children.

"You stay here, Fernando, and continue to work at your job."

Fernando bid a tearful good-bye to each of his children, then to his wife, and finally saw them off. The children waved farewell. They promised to write and visit often. The loss he felt wasn't due only to the coming separation, but to the realization that his children were changing so quickly he was afraid he would no longer recognize them.

Maria Isabel and Fernando left the future unspoken.

That afternoon his garden beckoned again, whispered for him to leave behind his troubles and seek solace where the past was preserved, only a few steps away.

In the days that followed, Fernando resumed the pace of daily life, going to work, paying bills, cooking his meals. But one day he found the entrance to a side street in the far corner of the yard. He wandered aimlessly down the street that seemed so hauntingly familiar. He turned up another street and, an hour or two later, stood facing the house where he had once lived in Horta, with two pigs in the yard—a fat one named Mussolini and a skinny one named Hitler. They had slaughtered these pigs to celebrate the end of the war and the end of those fascist leaders who had caused so much death and destruction. The plants in his San José yard thickened and spread; they did not form a typical veil but a dense impenetrable wall. Many bore the varieties of fruit that grew so plentifully on the islands—fruit he hadn't seen or tasted for several years. They hung down from the green canopy in clusters: *tomate capush, coração negro, cherimolia*, tiny sweet bananas, and *maracujá*.

Fernando settled in his lawn chair, surrounded by the stalks and tendrils of the garden. Now and again he reached up to pick a luscious piece of fruit.

He listened to the sea breezes, to the birds screaming in the wind, to the sound of waves crashing. He felt the sting of salt air and wandered like an old ghost through the mists, through his garden, through the narrow streets and buildings arrayed in the dimensions of an emerald island nestled in the mid-Atlantic.

He strolled the *avenida*, and stopped at the Café Internacional, to sit and argue the latest news with the other patrons. He glanced across to the Largo do Infante, where he had taken so many of his walks, and farther, to Horta's harbor, to Pico rising to the heavens, in the distance.

He tipped his hat to the storekeepers, "*Bom dia*, Senhor Machado," he said, smiling. Old friends and acquaintances walked past, offering their regards.

Here he would sit and paint to his heart's content, scenes that appeared before his eyes. He would write poems, too; for here were all the colors, sights, sounds, and smells he could never leave behind. Never again would he have to suffer *saudades* for all he longed for. Here he found only that which belonged to the Azores and nothing more.

He sat breathing in the air of Faial, as boats sailed in and out of the harbor. Life was good, things as they should be. Those distant unpleasant memories of another life, a life in another place—with no friends, no work, no Azores—he thankfully recognized as a bad dream—a fate that others suffered, perhaps, but not him.

His wife and children had gone on to find a better life, but the Azores contained all he wished for. After all, the islands were a part of him, as much as he was a part of them. He was no longer an exile. He had come home.

Eduardo's Promise

THE OLD WOMAN SCURRIED ACROSS THE SAND, BACK AND FORTH. EVERY now and then she would stop, bend down, and poke a stick at something in the sand. Occasionally, she picked up something of interest. Some children passed by on the road and shouted at her. They were too far away for her to make out what was said, but she had heard it all before: "What are you looking for, Mad Marisa? Treasure? Did you lose something? Your husband, maybe?" They repeated the words of their parents. She stood and waved. They laughed and she laughed back at them. She went back to her searching.

Finally she stopped and stared at something white jutting out of the sand. She circled it cautiously, as though it might suddenly spring at her. It was a bone.

"Well, well, what have we here," she said. "Some ancient sailor, perhaps?"

Looking around quickly, to make sure no one was watching, she bent down and picked it up. She turned the bone over, carefully examining both ends and along its length. The bone was large; most likely it had been a forearm, she thought.

She wrapped it in her shawl and carried it toward home, holding it in the crook of her arm, like a baby.

Everybody knew her as Marisa, the mad woman of Praia Negra, though Marisa wasn't her real name. They had called her that for so long that nobody could remember what her true name was, or even that the one they called her wasn't hers.

Some said she had always been mad, but most people believed it was losing her husband that drove her mad. Twenty years had passed since Eduardo had disappeared. Most believed he had left the islands and sailed off to Portugal or Madeira after a woman. There were rumors he had been seen years later.

Still, Marisa didn't believe any of them. "His boat was wrecked in a terrible storm. Everyone knows he was the best fisherman on the island. He always went farther than the others, and he brought back more fish than anyone else." Year after year she would tell people: "He'll come back. He said so. He made a promise. You'll see."

A few neighbors kept an eye on her, bringing her home if she got caught in the rain or lost. They left food for her and brought blankets and other household supplies. They had tried to talk her into leaving numerous times, to go to the mainland where she had family. But she refused. "This is where I belong," she said. "This is my home."

Every day Marisa left her small stone house and walked up and down the beach. She gazed out over the sea, studying the distance as though awaiting a sign, like the old whale watcher who sat in the lookout up the hill, peering constantly through the slits that served as a window with his pair of binoculars, ready to shoot off the flare announcing that he had sighted a whale in the distance.

She would return and walk in the other direction, combing the wet sand and the rocks for the odds and ends that occasionally washed ashore.

She never walked along the roads except when she went into the village for something. She didn't walk along the pastures or in the parks either, as though only the narrow strip of sand beckoned her: the thin border between the richly bountiful land of life, and that strange, living mystery out there, rippling with shadows, resounding with death.

After reaching her house, Marisa quickly rinsed the bone with water from the well. It was bleached white and spotless, but she scrubbed it nonetheless.

"Who are you?" she said, stepping inside and setting it down on the table. "Were you a sailor?" She lit a fire in the stove. "Or a fisherman who was washed overboard? Maybe someone killed you, pushed you off a ship. Or did you kill yourself by jumping into the sea?"

She brought out candles and set them on the table near the bone.

"Such great luck to have found you," she said. "Not just an ordinary find today. And how long have you been dead? Ah, who is to know such things? Maybe you are just some old pirate whose bones have finally washed up."

She didn't know where to put it. The bone was something special and didn't seem to belong with the other things she had found over the years—the bottles, rocks, bits of nets, and other debris which lined her windowsills and the shelf that held her dishes.

She left it on the table and examined it for a long time.

The next day she went out for much longer than she normally did, believing that perhaps she had overlooked another piece of bone, or that more had washed ashore during the night.

She didn't find anything, however—there were only the same old rocks, feathers, seaweed, and shells that always littered the sand. She left them alone, as though she couldn't be bothered by such ordinary things anymore.

Marisa came back home and began to worry about taking the bone.

"Oh, dear," she said. "What shall I do? Maybe it was happy where it was." She wondered if she should return the bone to where she had found it, thinking that maybe it was bad luck or disrespectful to disturb the dead. She didn't want to give it up, though. Perhaps, she thought, I should take it to the padre instead and have him bless it for me.

But the thought of having to re-bury the bone and the questions the padre might ask if she told him she wished to keep it only made her more confused.

Two days later, after a heavy downpour, she found another bone. It was shorter than the first one, but otherwise of the same solid, polished, and chalk-white material. She was overjoyed at the discovery.

"Two of them, and in such a short time, must be an omen!"

She took it straight home and placed it beside the other. She couldn't tell if they matched or belonged together, but she saw no other possibility; they had to be from the same unfortunate person.

The next day there was yet another bone, and the day after that several very small ones. She was terrified she might miss a piece and so she searched the area carefully, to make sure none had been overlooked.

Marisa laid them all together on the table, matching them, rearranging them, the larger ones on one side, the smaller ones on the other. She experimented, trying to fit them together.

She didn't always find the bones in the same spot, but they were never very far from one another, either. She wondered whether the sea washed the bones onto the shore, or if they were uncovered by shifting sands. She even thought that perhaps someone was leaving them for her to find, but that didn't seem possible. She never saw anyone else on the sand.

Sometimes she heard strains of an old song, mostly at night, but also during her walks in the daylight. But the sound was always faint and far away, drowned out by the crashing waves. During the storms, too, she heard it, like a frightened cat crying at the door to be let in.

"There is nothing very strange or unusual about a bone, perhaps," she said. "But bones that sing, well, that is something special, indeed."

It seemed like too much to ask for, to keep finding more bones, especially since she had already found such an extraordinary number of them. So she kept telling herself that there could not be any more, that she was only checking to make sure, and for no other reason than that. But they continued to appear nonetheless, each new find asking that she would return again.

Once she found an entire hand, lying as though it were reaching out for her. She found a flat piece of wood and carefully laid each bone in order upon the board.

Later she found several ribs, and hummed along as the bones sang to her, louder with each passing day.

In the evenings she sat and sewed. Occasionally she glanced at the arrangements of bones on the tabletop and was aware of an odd sensation, an unreasonable yet unshakable suspicion that grew with each additional piece of the skeleton. As it materialized she couldn't rid herself of the nagging feeling of familiarity; each piece was like a flavor she had tasted long ago, a word she had once heard spoken and which still echoed.

Often, as she hung up her clothes to dry or worked in her garden, she found herself trembling, unable to shut out the growing realization, the sensations that seized her like the flush of a high fever.

In another week she had finished putting one of the legs together, and then she knew: there was no longer any doubt in her mind—this was her husband's rib, his leg, his skeleton she was piecing together.

"Eduardo," she cried, holding one of the ribs in her hand. "I knew you would come back. Piece by piece, across hundreds or thousands of miles after twenty long years. I know now why these bones seemed so precious to me!"

She held each of them, kissed them one by one, whispering her forgiveness. Whenever there was a break or a pause between storms, she returned carrying more bones to add to the growing skeleton. When the rain was unrelenting it was most difficult. She couldn't stop thinking about what new piece, if any, awaited her, and after looking repeatedly at the bones, she would finally cover them with a blanket and try to think of something else.

She was nagged by constant fears that there would be no more. If two days went by with no new bones, she worried, and she knew she couldn't possibly live through another day.

While she kept busy collecting and assembling his bones, she felt more alive than she had felt in years. She sang as she worked in the garden and smiled happily as she roamed through the hallways and kitchen, listening as the song of the bones filled the house. The sun shone brighter, and the sea seemed to laugh and dance, sharing her joy. It was as if he were courting her all over again. She remembered Eduardo's glances and his halting words as he had attempted to win her heart, the way her love for him had grown and their dreams had become one.

With each passing day she learned more about how he should be put together, where each piece belonged. It was painstaking work, like a jigsaw puzzle in which she could see a picture slowly taking shape.

She pieced his other hand together. "How those very hands used to hold mine," she said, stroking the long, narrow fingers.

The villagers walked past her house and shook their heads. "Listen," she would hear them say to one another. "Mad Marisa talking to herself. Poor thing!"

"But see, she's smiling too. She's crazy, yes, but she's also happy."

Just after the second leg was completed, the bones stopped coming. She spent the whole afternoon the next day looking, gasping for breath and straining her brittle lungs, but came home empty-handed and exhausted.

"My God!" she cried, "To have a half-finished husband! Please, let the rest come."

The next day she looked, mad with fever, burning in her quest to find a piece, any piece, just something to add, something to keep him coming.

She went home convinced it was over, wondering how she could go on. For two days she lay in bed weak and afraid, reluctant to get up and look at him, scared of going to the shore and finding nothing.

There were several more days of rain, and she did little but pace around the house, checking on him again and again, waiting impatiently to go search the beach. In the evenings she sat eating stale bread and homemade cheese, listening to the screams and shrieks, the cries of the wind lashing and pounding against the house, as though the storms were intent on clearing everything off the island. She would hum or sing along with Eduardo, whose resonant voice calmed and reassured her.

On the day following the storm she woke early. The skies were bright and clear. She bundled warmly and went out. It was there, waiting for her, almost as if someone had carefully left it where she was sure to find it: his skull.

"My husband," she said, holding his skull lovingly in her hands. "Yes, I would certainly recognize you anywhere."

Now that he was almost complete, she moved him. She put him into his own bed, which still stood beside hers. He lay upon the top sheet, perfectly at peace.

In the nights she looked over, even though she knew he was there, next to her.

He looked better, as each passing day he came to life, stronger, purer, as though he had been distilled, and now only the essentials remained. All the excess, the fancies, the faults and weaknesses of being a man had been stripped away. Time and the terrible ordeal he'd gone through, the long periods of solitude, had made a new man of him.

She sat for several hours every day and talked to him while she knitted a new shawl, telling him about everything that had happened in his absence, the events and circumstances of her life alone, as though she wanted no space, no doubts or shadows, no misunderstandings or secrets between them.

Occasionally, she scolded him for his carelessness, for his foolishness. "Just like a man! To go off, leave your home and family, with no one to look after you, and end up getting yourself killed. It's a terrible thing!"

Later, as if to make up to him, she brought out a dish of oil and smoothed it on him with a cloth, bone by bone, polishing each until he was radiant.

She held his head in her hands and peered into his sockets, seeing the vast depths of the oceans and feeling the implacable pull of those distant currents. "It's like listening to a seashell," she said. "Such distances and depths, which I can see instead of hear. Tell me, then, what happened to you? Where were you all those years?"

And she sat and listened to the whisper like the sea wind cutting through the rigging of the sails, telling her of the endless days at sea, the boat blown off course, the desolation and the fear, the hunger and the dehydration, and later the storm, water rushing everywhere, and finally, the boat going down.

"I know. I told them all," Marisa said. "I missed you, and to have you back again—it's a miracle!" She wiped the tears off his skull, and smiled triumphantly.

She began making a new dress. "My wedding dress," she said, holding it up. She made him lunch and dinner, taking care to fix Eduardo's favorite meals, and brought him wine when he asked for some. It made her happy to hear him sing or whistle. "Sounds as though the house is filled with birds," she said happily.

"Tell me," she sometimes said. "What will we do?" And he would tell her of the boat he would build, how they would leave the island and sail together the way they should have done. "Ah, yes, a honeymoon, just like you promised."

She smiled, knowing he meant it, and she couldn't doubt it would happen, not after he had come so far to be with her again.

~ ~ ~

It was *Semana do Mar*—the Week of the Sea. Every year a great procession would make its way toward the ocean and the seafarer's church. Most of the town gathered, all finely dressed and singing. Some of the children wore white veils upon their heads, and held flowers. The men carried musical instruments, a staff or a cross, and, at the end, the figure of the saint and the infant, high upon their shoulders. Marisa never missed the celebrations.

Stopping a group of youngsters on their way to join the crowd, she had them drag Eduardo's dory down to the strand. When they had left, she placed a soft mat on the bottom and laid Eduardo out on it, making sure that he was comfortable. She covered him with his only suit.

When the people saw her rowing through the waves towards the church, they shouted and pointed. They hushed as several men ran out into the surf to help her to shore. Marisa stood, proud of her beautiful wedding shawl, and showed them how neatly she had placed Eduardo's bones. "My husband has come back for me," said Marisa.

Marisa heard a mad flutter as the villagers raised their hands to cross themselves and whisper a prayer to Our Lady. One woman screamed. The padre quickly blessed Eduardo and Marisa and said a prayer. The villagers whispered: "What can this mean? How is such a thing possible?"

"God has seen fit to bring them together," one neighbor said. Several others spoke up in agreement.

The padre nodded sympathetically. "Clearly this is God's wish. He alone could have brought Eduardo back to her."

The crowd buzzed with the miracle that had taken place. The children filled the boat with flowers. The villagers began walking slowly, many barefoot, holding lighted candles, toward the whalemen's church. Marisa asked to follow the procession in her dory.

One of the neighbors helped her through the surf and returned to the procession along the beach, while the *guitarras* and the horns played sweetly.

As the procession arrived at its destination, Eduardo reached up, set the small sail, and headed out for the open sea.

A few of the villagers started running to another boat, as if to bring her back, but Marisa saw the priest restrain them and raise his hand in benediction.

Ah, thought Marisa, *the good priest understands.* She wove the flowers into her hair and waved good-bye from the back of the boat.

Eduardo sailed a perfect course away from the island, until it disappeared from Marisa's view. His song had ended. Now there was only the sound of the wind in the sail and the sea breaking against the small boat.

The Saint of Quebrado do Caminho

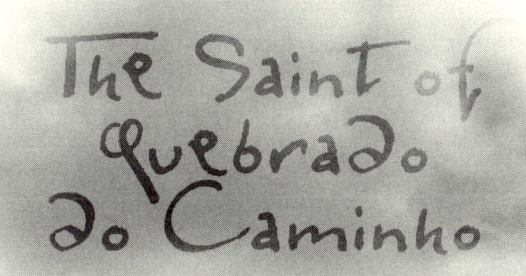

CONSTANTINO MALDONADO GAZED DOWN AT THE WOMAN BELOW HIM with prolonged embarrassment, at a complete loss to explain how, now that their lovemaking was over, he couldn't uncouple himself. Though he struggled, they couldn't separate.

He laughed a very halfhearted laugh.

"Just one moment," he said, squirming, trying to get away.

The woman, her eyes growing wide with fear and incomprehension, began trying to push him away. Constantino tried to rise, straining and inhaling the stale breath of the woman, the odor of garlic and onions lingering, as she panted from the exertion of trying to free herself.

It was no use. They were stuck fast.

"How in the devil?" Constantino asked.

The young woman panicked. "What if someone finds us?" she said. "My mother. She will soon be home! What will we do?"

"Relax," he ordered soberly. "It's the only way." They both made a great effort to relax, and Constantino tried to roll off the woman. Then they twisted, turned and struggled, but no matter what they did they were unsuccessful in breaking free of one another.

She began to cry. "What has happened? What will I do? What have you done to me?"

What a fix, he thought. She sobbed quietly, as if afraid of upsetting him. Her dark, work-roughened skin contrasted sharply with Constantino's fair, almost pale complexion.

Why had he come here to Quebrado do Caminho, involving himself with a woman this far beneath him? She was just a poor country girl, after all, a peasant who didn't know anything beyond her own village, how to wring a chicken's neck, or milk goats. What did she know about music, poetry, the world, life? He couldn't very well go back to Horta and let his friends see them together. He'd be the laughingstock. But, then, how could he remain here, too, where he would also be exposed to ridicule and humiliation?

Here he was, a man of education—an aristocrat, if not exactly wealthy—quite literally stuck to an ignorant girl—a most embarrassing situation—unable to free himself, when all he wanted was to be as far away from her as possible.

At any moment the girl's mother would arrive home, find them together, and then what?

The girl, Maria Joaquina, amid all the twisting about, shoving, and pushing, kept gathering up the sheets in a futile attempt to cover herself.

"What are you doing?" he said.

"Do you think I want the whole world to see?"

"Unless you let me go everyone will soon know, regardless."

"Me?"

"Yes, you."

"I'm not doing this."

"Well it's not me," he said.

They heard the sound of the door to the house open and shut, and then the steady tap-tapping of Maria Joaquina's mother's hard-soled shoes on the floor. She called her daughter's name, and the girl choked back a cry. The woman came toward the room where the two lovers lay, and pushed open the door. There was a sudden gasp and the instantaneous flutter of her hands rising, imploring toward heaven, "Oh, Our Lady!" the woman shrieked. "In my own house!" Her hands sketched the sign of the cross several times. "Oh, dear Mother of God!" She covered her eyes and turned away but then just as quickly turned around once again, facing the man and her daughter joined in their moment of sin. "Get out, you!" she shouted, pointing her finger at Constantino. "Get out!"

Maria Joaquina continued grabbing at the sheet—covering one part, then exposing another, and so on—while the man to whom she was joined attempted to calm the two women down.

"Please, please, senhora, this will do none of us any good."

The mother's lips didn't cease their motions as she raised a litany of curses and invocations. "How could you do this to my little child, my helpless innocent? Tempter! Devil! You, with all your fine airs and fancy talk. Seducer!"

She came toward them threateningly. "May your children have club feet and be idiots!" Quite possibly she realized that any child they might have would be her grandchild, for she suddenly stopped cursing the unborn, but continued to heap a steady stream of abuse upon the two before her.

The old woman turned toward her daughter, who shook in fear, clutching the sheets and mopping up her tears.

"You tramp!" she shouted. "A fine bitch in heat. Such sin! Never, in all my years. Will you be happy, now, that they'll be dragging our name through the streets?" She turned an imploring and apologetic look up to heaven. "Right here in front of God!"

"Senhora," the man, pleaded, "Dona Celestina." He explained to the woman their unfortunate circumstance as best he could, and urged her to be sensible and go out and find them a doctor. Finally, the woman, without a word, got up and left.

She came back an hour or so later with an old country man who called himself a doctor—though most sensible people never referred to him as such, or trusted him to diagnose anything more serious than a headache or cold. He was an ugly, heavyset man, who sweated profusely, and was generally considered a pompous ass by his friends and neighbors. Regardless, he was still the only one who even remotely passed for a doctor on that side of the island. One went to real doctors and hospitals—which people called slaughterhouses—only to die.

The doctor entered the house unable to understand what all the fuss was about, why this mad woman had dragged him out of his chair and away from his *aguardente* and brought him here. Once he saw for himself, however, he found this most singular situation particularly intriguing. "This is the most interesting case I have seen in all my years of doctoring," he said, trying to stifle a laugh. "I have waited all my life for just such a case!" He took down copious notes in a worn black booklet, wanting to know all the particulars: how long they had been like that, how long their coupling had been, how they had attempted to extricate themselves, so far.

"*So!*" the mother asked. "What are you going to do about this?"

After a thorough examination, the doctor stood up and exclaimed: "There is only one way I know of to solve this problem."

"Hurry man, hurry," Constantino said.

The doctor left the room with Senhora Celestina; they returned carrying several buckets of cold water, which they threw onto the couple, who screamed and cursed, but were still stuck fast together, shivering from the cold.

"Well?" Senhora Celestina said to the doctor.

"I'm afraid, senhora, there is nothing more I can do."

"But will they go on like this then, forever?"

"That is difficult to say. Perhaps they will, uh,"—he coughed—"separate in time. Or, perhaps . . . ?" He shrugged, as if to leave that question to their imagination.

"There must be something that can be done," Constantino said, impatient and even more irritated after being drenched.

"Maybe," the mother suggested, "a specialist is what is needed. Senhor Guapo just might know what is best in a condition like this."

"You mean the veterinarian?" the doctor said with a snort. "What does he know? Cows, horses, yes—but this is another matter. For this you need a medical specialist. Someone from the mainland."

However, no one seemed interested in bringing in an outsider, and besides, finding a person from another island or the mainland would take time. Joaquina's mother insisted that the vet was a sensible and practical man, who more than once had proved to be more capable than fancy specialists. "It's worth a try," Constantino said.

Later in the day the vet came—a wiry, dried-out husk of a man, who looked as if he were made of corn stalks. He reeked of horse dung and cow's milk. He pondered over what to do, gave several puzzled exclamations. He squirmed and shifted round in his seat, changing his position every few minutes, as if uncomfortable with himself, unsure what to do with his arms and legs.

"Well!" the mother said.

"I must be alone with them for a moment," he answered.

She left the room and the good vet went to work. He was a man who had had much experience in the ways of cattle and sheep, goats and horses, and had even helped to deliver a child once or twice, but this was something completely beyond his simple expertise and experience. They had no luck, and after some time he came out rubbing the side of his face.

"I'm sorry," he said, shrugging, and leaving the house with his tail between his legs.

"Imbecile," said the mother.

So Constantino and this young, unrefined girl—the daughter of a poor and simple farmhand who one day had sighed deeply at the futility of his life, gave up, and died—made the best of it. They shut themselves up in their room, hidden away from the world.

On occasion the old woman still tried to come between them, to pull them apart, but it did no good. She created various medicinal concoctions, which she felt might somehow facilitate their separation, burning rosemary to ward off any lingering evils, and making them ingest teas brewed with bitter-tasting roots and berries.

Word spread around the village and people came by to have a look at the impossible, though the mother quickly shooed them away, calling them names and insulting each and every one of their ancestors. "Go on, you busybodies," she said. "Keep your noses where they belong. Let a poor family suffer in peace."

Senhora Celestina quietly prayed for them both, as well as for the child she soon learned would be born—after the doctor confirmed her suspicions. She lamented their sin, their shame, and their fate. Her husband had died and left her with nothing but problems—and now this. Who could have put this terrible curse upon her family? Things like this couldn't happen without someone wishing evil upon one of them, or the entire family.

"We must get you married," she informed the couple—always referring to them in the singular now—"right away. I will call Father Alves. At least that way God may be tolerant with us and spare this house from any more catastrophes."

What could they say or do? The girl's mother fashioned an outfit for them, covering that part which needed covering, and disguising their plight, so that they almost looked like two separate people.

Father Alves came. Blind as a bat, he didn't even notice the peculiar arrangement of the couple, their unusual closeness. "It's good to see two people who love each other so much," he said, smiling fondly. "Yes, yes," Senhora Celestina said, as she rushed the priest into performing the ceremony. Father Alves blessed them both, jovial at the happy union of such a pair and commenting warmly on how well it boded for their future happiness.

The couple were quickly pronounced man and wife.

At moments Constantino attempted to be philosophical about his fate. "Perhaps I am overlooking the true significance of this situation," he said to himself one night, as Joaquina slept. He mulled the idea over and over. "Here

I am, trapped, in a sense, chained, to this poor ignorant child. Could there be some reason for this?" The cause persistently eluded him and yet he followed, hunting its trail and trying repeatedly to pin it down. He had never heard of anyone in his family suffering the same fate, and so he doubted that it had been inherited from his side.

Still, shadows of doubts came treading, unbidden and troubling, upon these moments of reflection, begging at the doors of his consciousness, easily gaining a foot in the door. "Then again, it could all be some trick conjured by the two of them, mother and daughter. What do I know about them? Nothing. Perhaps the grandmother was a *benzedeira* of this village. This may all be witchcraft, fashioned to take advantage of my position, my name, my aristocracy."

On the other hand, he knew he had taken advantage of the girl's innocence and naïveté. Perhaps God was punishing him for his sins?

He stared out the window at the stark landscape of Pico. The mountain was shrouded in its usual gloomy cloak of unrelenting clouds; the sea whispered and its waves eternally winked, as if gratefully passing on to more interesting climes. Fifteen miles out to sea, the shadowy mountain range of São Jorge loomed above the water. Constantino sighed the helpless sigh that was becoming a recurring sigh of resignation. He believed that the mass of rock before him—the cooled remnant of a molten volcanic thrust through the earth's crust—along with the green vines and fields, the whitewashed houses and stone buildings, even the cows, that all these were conspiratorially mocking his plight.

He was brought back to the here and now by the voice of the woman to whom he was stuck, asking him whether he thought the baby would be a boy or a girl, or if their predicament might somehow adversely affect the child. Again he sighed, wondering why it was that even the sound of her voice so irritated him now.

Joaquina grew with the child at an incredible rate, becoming as large and round in days what normally would have taken months. To Constantino's horror, he found himself suffering some of the same symptoms as she. Whenever the girl burst into tears, so would he. When she felt tired and slept for hours and hours, he would do the same. He shared her many aches and pains, the same cramps and pressures. The two of them together were a pitiful sight.

They felt depressed about the same things, fought with Maria Joaquina's mother about the same things, and were swept along together by every stray emotion under the sun. The baby rolled round and round between them the whole while, while the parents resembled two ruffled, squawking birds, each struggling to sit on the same egg.

But they didn't always feel in unison, didn't always have the same desires. One might wish to take a walk, the other to sit. One might want to face a certain way as they slept, while the other would wish to face in the opposite direction, or not to sleep at all. These disagreements only caused more problems.

"This is unnatural, as everyone has said," Joaquina complained. "Only the devil could make two people stick together like this. Everyone in the village believes the devil himself caused this."

Constantino ignored his young wife's outburst. Instead he pondered how the child would be born, with the added complication of himself being somewhat in the way. He couldn't very well trouble his wife with unanswerable questions, even though she asked herself the same things, and kept him awake during the night.

Sometimes he would respond to her talk of the devil. "It was God's doing," he would say. "Only God could think of something as dreadful as this!" But she failed to find his attempt at a joke humorous.

As Joaquina's belly grew with the child, life became much more uncomfortable for them both. Even the most ordinary of mundane acts became nearly impossible.

Constantino longed for the days when he had met with friends, talked and joked, read and composed verses for the ladies. He longed for the days when he could be alone. He wondered if he would ever return to the simple, unfettered joys of those times. If Joaquina and her mother could care for the child, after it was born, perhaps then he would be free and could flee to Horta, to see to business matters . . .

On top of everything else, he continuously wondered whether the child really was his. Lately, he had become more and more convinced that he was in fact the innocent victim of these two women's malevolent witchcraft or ingenious fraud.

One day Joaquina proclaimed that she was giving up the material life, that henceforth she would devote her life to serving God. "My child will be a child of God," she said. "We will serve God together."

"First it's the devil, now God. Besides, you are married," Constantino argued.

"I cannot be a nun," she said with sadness. "But I can still devote myself to God."

Her mind seemed made up. Still, to Constantino it seemed a strange thing, given their unusual circumstances. He felt a trifle bothered, besides, that she had all these thoughts about God and the devil, and did not seem to appreciate who her child would have for a father and be thankful for that fact.

"You could have done far worse than me for a husband," he said.

"Some husband," Joaquina said. "You cannot right a wrong simply by marrying me."

Sometimes, while Constantino snored loudly, Joaquina read verses from her mother's Bible, reciting her prayers, making promises and offering sacrifices to the saints.

Constantino tried to sleep as much as possible, hoping to wake up one day and find himself a free man again. His laziness irritated his wife and mother-in-law.

"Any good husband would be doing something to provide for his family," Joaquina's mother said. "Look at you sleeping your life away, living here like a prince."

"Like a prince, you say!" Constantine shouted. "No, not like a prince, but like a prisoner."

Joaquina too found fault with her husband's behavior. "You are not setting a good example for our child. There are many things we will need. How will you provide for me, and the child? Besides, it wouldn't do you any harm to pray as well. Maybe the child won't grow up as lazy as his father."

Constantino prayed, but only that the ordeal would end, that he could resume his unencumbered life of style and comfort, chasing the pretty girls of Horta. "I've learned my lesson," he cried, though he couldn't have said what the lesson was. Then he closed his eyes and resumed sleeping.

Little things began magnifying and multiplying, becoming large enough to annoy each other.

"You sweat too much, and smell."

"It is the smell of a man," Constantino said. "Don't ask me to apologize for that."

And when he touched her: "Your hands," she complained. "They feel rough like the bark of an old tree."

"And you, with that, that enormous thing sticking out from your stomach!"

"I never should have married you, brute!" she said.

"Bah! I'd walk out of here if I could!" he said.

"And I would send you packing if I could."

And so it went, on and on, day and night.

The disaster occurred one day after Joaquina's mother had left for a neighboring village, to visit her ailing sister.

Joaquina, according to her own testimony, had shut herself in her room, feeling that the birth of the child was imminent, and that she should devote all her time and strength to prayer, in the hopes that God would smile kindly upon the child and protect it from harm.

Two days later, just before Joaquina's mother was to return home, her neighbors were alerted to strange and disturbing sounds coming from inside the house. Two women went up to the door and pounded, but no one answered. Fearing that, in Senhora Celestina's absence, Joaquina might have fallen and hurt herself, or that some complication had arisen concerning her pregnancy, the women opened the door and entered—to find Joaquina in labor. One of the women went for the doctor.

The doctor took over, sending the women to fetch him water and towels, and ordering everyone else out of the house.

It was at this moment that Joaquina's mother arrived.

The house was in crisis, with everybody scrambling to be of some use, or to inquire about Joaquina and her child, or Joaquina's poor old mother.

The doctor, with Senhora Celestina's assistance, delivered the baby; both Joaquina and son were fine, normal. Things quieted down in the house. The mother was the first to notice her son-in-law's disappearance. She was furious.

"Where is he?" each person asked the other, amazed to find that no one had noticed his absence earlier. "Where has he gone?" Questions were asked of everyone outside the house, but no one had seen him.

"I knew he was no good, that he would leave her the first chance he got," Dona Celestina said.

When Joaquina herself was finally questioned about her husband, she couldn't answer. "I don't know," she said. "I can't remember."

A thorough search was conducted but turned up nothing. A week later the authorities came to the house to investigate. The doctor was summoned, as were the neighbors who had found Joaquina, along with the priest and even the veterinarian. Joaquina answered their questions as best she could, though she remembered very little—only that she had stayed in the room to pray after her mother had left to visit Joaquina's aunt, and that her husband, Constantino, had been asleep most of that time. The next thing she remembered was the searing agony of labor, and then the neighbors coming in.

The investigation proved fruitless, and no trace of Constantino was ever found, nor any explanation for his disappearance. There was another examination, some months later, when someone maliciously suggested to the police, in an anonymous note, that Joaquina, in a fit, had stabbed Constantino and buried him in the yard. The matter was quickly dropped, after a thorough and fruitless search of the yard was conducted. "No woman in her condition could have been capable of such an action," the chief of police said, wiping his hands of the matter.

As time passed the stories grew more wild and fantastic, attaining the status of legends in and around Quebrado do Caminho and the neighboring town of Santa Luzia. It was said that Joaquina's mother had put a disappearing spell upon her son-in-law; that Constantino himself was employed by the devil and had left to continue his dirty work elsewhere; it was even suggested that Joaquina had taken to cannibalism and eaten the poor man, then fashioned a crib for the baby with the bones of her dead husband.

No one in Horta ever saw or heard from Constantino either, leading the puzzled investigators to scratch their heads in confusion. It was as if he had never existed. All traces of him began to disappear as well. Those questioned would sit back and examine their memories, then shrug, having come back empty-handed, unable to recollect anything concerning the mysterious Constantino Maldonado, other than that they were sure they had heard of him, or that his name was familiar.

In fact, the only trace left anywhere of Constantino was in the child who bore his name, and in his widow's daily prayers.

Joaquina wasted no time in assuming the part, dressing in black, clutching her rosary, and living a quiet life with her son, who was rumored to be a quiet, dreamy boy with light features like his father, and who reportedly studied very diligently to become a priest. No one could say for sure, however, since Joaquina never let the boy out of her sight, keeping him safely tucked away within her mother's house, as if afraid that he too might disappear.

And this is how one of the poorest souls in all of Pico, Maria Joaquina, came to be regarded as the Saint of Quebrado do Caminho.

Night Magic

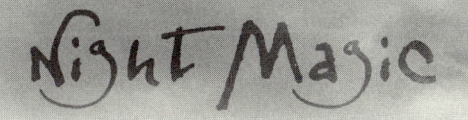

MISFORTUNE FOLLOWED GASPAR HENRIQUES RELENTLESSLY, NO matter where he went.

There was something that kept people from looking into Gaspar's eyes, an uneasiness they felt, which made them turn away. He was a composite of artificial limbs and missing pieces, of replacements and scars. He drew misfortune from the most unlikely places. After losing an eye in a fight while visiting the island of Flores, he accepted a glass replacement with his customary resignation to what life proffered. Applying his own personal sense of whimsy and decorum, he painted a landscape scene in miniature upon the new eyeball, tinted, of course, in blue because, "That's how I now wish to view the world."

Gaspar was rootless. He was born on the island of Pico, raised on Faial until his late teens, then dragged by his parents to America, where he learned English, joined the Air Force, and became an American. But after many years working at a Portuguese newspaper, and an unsuccessful marriage, he decided he didn't belong in America, so he packed up and left for Europe. After eight months of roaming from one end of Europe to the other, he left. Traveling by boat, he drifted from country to country, from place to place, tried his hand at any number of jobs, to say nothing of relationships with women of every type, every color, every nationality imaginable.

After several years of this he finally ended up back in the Azores, on the island of Pico. He'd arranged to stay in a building that belonged to a family who owed him a favor. It was little more than a stone hut.

There he settled. He had a cow, a few chickens, a couple of pigs, and a scraggly old cat named Fofinho. He grew his own vegetables and fruit. His needs, he found, were few and simple.

The people on Pico referred to him as the American, although he hardly considered himself as such. He had thought that perhaps he was a European, but he never found a place that could claim him. Part of the purpose of his travels was to find somewhere he felt he belonged. That was why he had come back to the Azores, where he had begun life. The volcano, he decided, was a part of him, and he of it.

They accused him of possessing more lives than any one single person had a right to possess. As a result, they felt even more uneasy around him. Nevertheless, Gaspar rode through life as if he were subject to the vicissitudes of the waves and the winds. He possessed a light-hearted recklessness, an exuberance and abandon that ultimately couldn't help but find expression in the ever-evolving map of carelessness, the weathering, the deep grooves and lines of misfortune that repeatedly marred his physical appearance.

Though he wasn't much to look at, some compared him to Magellan, whose nose, it is said, was broken in some forgotten brawl, who bore scars of battle and walked with a pronounced limp, the souvenir of a lance wound in Morocco.

"I guess I'm just a patchwork man," Gaspar joked, after losing a gangrenous leg, only to replace it with part of a spar from a nineteenth-century sailing ship. "I want something of the earth, no man-made contraption, no machine, but wood, solid, true."

It delighted him to no end that the painted orb which replaced his lost eye tinged everything with a fine blue tint.

"Life is a game meant to be played," he would say. "And I carry the proof that I have played it too well."

Gaspar had long since given up on trying to figure out the hows and whys of a world that continuously broke its own natural laws.

He had survived more scrapes, more close calls, more broken bones, more narrow misses—miracles, really—than anyone could possibly count.

Still, he was a man of boundless energy. I say *was* because, as far as the world was concerned, his supply of lives had run out. If he was no longer among the living, then he could no longer worry anybody who still was. No one would have to wonder whether he was about to use up what any decent person spent in one brief and uneventful lifetime, or worse still, become filled with the apprehension that, through his own unfailing misfortune, he would bring disaster crashing down upon other heads as well.

He was seen as a man who lived in a different mode than others. He seemed to burn brighter, hotter—not that he sought danger, really. He did not live a life of excess, by any means, but rather as if he'd been born with one foot already in the grave.

Again I say *was* because when someone vanishes without a trace, when he isn't seen or heard from, the world tends to conclude, after a spell, that the person is dead. But then, what does the world know?

He'd always been extremely thin. People claimed that when he stood sideways he neatly vanished from sight. More than once he'd gotten himself out of a sticky situation by performing contortions that for anyone else would have been physically impossible. Gaspar Henriques was built in a way that made it possible to bend without breaking, to form odd angles at any point on his body, to conform to whatever circumstances required.

He also was very nearly transparent. It seemed that any strong gust of wind would take him, especially if he flattened himself out in a conscious act of dissipating, blending into his surroundings like the chameleon he was, his bones often pulling free of their sockets, his extremities left dangling comically until Gaspar or someone else properly relocated the loose arm or leg.

Gaspar had traveled through all parts of the world: he'd been swept overboard in the Indian Ocean and lost in the Amazon. He had trekked through Nepal, island-hopped through the South Pacific, and crisscrossed Africa numerous times.

Along the way he had encountered various disasters and emergencies. He had been operated on, several times, by native tribesmen, who saved him from ailments that ranged from poisonous snakebites to tropical diseases, drownings to tumors. It was said that he'd had an organ or two removed, that these had been replaced with various implants—including a fibrous plant in one case and several animal parts—miraculously without suffering any sort of rejection or infection.

He lost a finger in a fight with a drunk outside a bar in Tangiers. A woman who watched as the drunk was being dragged away reportedly picked up the finger and ran off, believing it contained mystical powers; it continued to wiggle months, even years afterwards. She kept the finger in an earthenware jar, attempting, when she brought it out, to read the cryptic meanings of its persistent gestures.

After each of his trials and ordeals, against either man or a calloused nature which seemed hell-bent on destroying him, there was less and less that remained of Gaspar Henriques.

"I am merely being honed down to a fine edge," he would say, raising his shoulders as if to suggest this was Fate, with whom no one could argue.

Most animals—except, strangely enough, marine mammals and birds—would have nothing to do with him.

People too shied away, kept their distance. One felt inexplicable things in his presence, troubling waves radiated outward, leaving a wake of disturbances: people suddenly found tears welling in their eyes, a lump in their throats, a dogged sadness biting at their heels.

Indeed, Gaspar came to believe that if he simply stayed put somewhere, disaster would soon follow—hurricanes, floods, tornados, and fires, leaving him in ruins perhaps, but alive nonetheless.

"I've witnessed more disasters than the Bible," he often told people.

Gaspar merely picked himself up afterward and moved on to the next place, wherever he could hop aboard a ship, or a train, or catch a ride farther down the road. Once, when swept out to sea and half-drowned by a hurricane off the island of Flores, Gaspar held on to the fin of a dolphin, which safely guided him back to shore.

He had scars everywhere and pieces missing here and there, all of which truly did make him look like a patchwork man, not all too well stuck together.

∽ ∽ ∽

Gaspar Henriques spoke at great length with the dead; he knew many of their first names as well as their likes, dislikes, habits, and hobbies. The little cemetery at Quebrado do Caminho was a park where he came to enjoy their company. The dead provided welcome companionship in his otherwise bleak solitude—glimmers of light in the descending darkness of the failing vision of his remaining eye.

It struck him as magnificently odd and wondrous that, after some fifty years (he didn't know the exact date of his birth) of wandering back and forth over the surface of the planet, marriage and children, a lifetime of various relationships, that this tiny patch of ground was the place he had been aiming for all along.

No one could possibly have guessed that the often strange trajectory of his life would land him here in the tiny cemetery in Quebrado do Caminho, on the island of Pico, in the Azores.

"Why do you spend so much time here?" Mariana Antonia dos Reis—born in 1857, died in 1894—asked him.

"To keep alive memories," he answered. "Perhaps we can keep each other alive after a fashion."

He watched the sun edging nearer the horizon through Mariana's left eye. It was a breathtaking sight.

"It is good that you like it here," Rosa said. "Otherwise my poor husband wouldn't know what to do with himself." They laughed. Rosa and Miguel's marriage had continued to season well after their deaths, but it was true that Miguel was Gaspar's special comrade, helping him along with sturdy arms and legs and two good eyes, taking a keen interest in his life, which was the one last link Miguel maintained with the world of the living. But more than this, Miguel and the others found that, in listening to Gaspar, they experienced things they wouldn't otherwise have seen, smelled, tasted, or heard—things that Gaspar somehow made real with his stories of explorers and sailors, of star-crossed lovers and brave adventurers.

"There's no place I'd rather be and no better company," Gaspar said.

"No?" Mariana said. "Aren't there girls in the town you talk to?"

"Whose perfume you can breathe?" Rosa said.

"Whose eyes you can gaze upon," Miguel said with a heavy sigh, gazing up toward the stars. "And whose hands you can hold."

"No, I'm afraid not. Like so many things in the world of today, for me they are a monumental disappointment. For all their perfumes and substance, they are far more invisible than you, and I don't exist much for them either. We don't seem to share much in common. It's as if we are from different worlds. They peer straight through me."

Mariana smiled.

"Besides, they don't hold a candle to you," he said softly.

He winked and rose as Miguel came to his side.

"You are going already?" Mariana asked.

"Yes. I'll be back, though. I promise. Till tomorrow."

"Till tomorrow," Mariana said.

Assisted by Miguel, Gaspar left the graveyard, limping on his one good leg, the other with its worn but solid wood and metal fittings trembling with each step, as if longing to take root in the soil beneath his feet; the parts of him which were flesh and blood edged nearer to uselessness, increasingly unable to accommodate him in his changing world. Gaspar returned to his room, rented in the house of old Luisa Figueiredo.

He had absolutely no idea how he had returned to this place. Quebrado do Caminho, after all, was a long way from Los Angeles, where he last remembered being, though he could no longer say when that had been. Things merely happened, more frequently since his eyes went bad. Gaspar had been forced to leave his job after he lost the leg and his vision began to fail.

There'd been times when he saw nothing, when he would navigate by smell and some innate sense of air currents and pressures. Other times he saw more than the surface appearance, farther, deeper, than eyes were ever meant to see.

He remembered growing up in Quebrado when he was a boy. He'd dreamed for many years of returning. To this place, where time had nothing at all to do with clocks, and where he didn't have to constantly assure himself that anything was possible, for it was demonstrated all around him. The disability check he received went a lot farther in the Azores. Here his needs were simpler, he could find peace of mind, recollect his thoughts—scattered memories and dream fragments—into something that resembled order. It was almost as though he was simply where he should be, where he had to be. As if he could not exist anywhere else.

"It's okay to have only one leg," Gaspar explained to the sullen ghost by his side. "The more parts I lose, the stronger I become."

"How is that?" Miguel asked.

"It's a matter of concentrating one's powers. The less of me there is, the more potent what remains becomes. If I lose a finger, the life, the energy, doesn't remain with the finger, but relocates instead in the hand, making the hand even stronger. Anyway, it's a theory of mine."

The ghost nodded somewhat less than convincingly.

"That and the art of opening up new possibilities, new ways of seeing, utilizing other senses."

Something had to explain the extreme variations of time and place, of sight and sound, which were now such an integral part of his life. What should be wasn't, and what was hitherto impossible, no longer was.

"How did you lose your leg?"

"By forgetting about it for too long."

"And the old woman—will she be angry?"

"It's okay, Miguel. She is becoming used to me. I'm like an adopted son to her. She only feels she is helping out by insisting I get out of the house, that I make friends."

"You have many friends, senhor."

"Yes, Miguel. The best of friends, too."

The ghost led the nearly blind man down the road towards the house. "You should see the stars tonight, senhor."

"I can, Miguel. I see them beautifully. Part of me is up there." He nodded his head at the evening sky. "I am proof that someone can be in many places at the same time. That, I believe, is the true meaning of the word *saudade*. Not being parted from something, but being torn apart yourself, having parts of you missing, for being with someone or somewhere far away.

"That could be why we Portuguese are known for our sadness," Miguel said.

"Perhaps. With so many Portuguese spread all over the world, it means there are so many with parts of themselves left somewhere else."

They approached the house and Miguel turned to his friend. "Senhor, what if the old lady asks you where you've been? Will you tell her?"

"No, don't worry. I'll tell her I was at a café. That will keep her pleased. She doesn't need to know how bad things are."

"No."

"She doesn't understand the way things are. There is no need to hide from the future any more than from the past. In the graveyard they are all one; after all, you don't refuse a newcomer to the soil, do you?"

"No, we all get along, and no one is more or less than his or her neighbor. Even ancient enemies find ways to lose the cause of their disputes."

"And that's the way it should be. The living could certainly take a few lessons from the dead, if you ask me. It would be a far better world."

"She is afraid for you, senhor."

"Yes, but I've been with this too long to be afraid anymore."

They walked up the steps of the house. Inside, they were greeted by the rich smells of dinner cooking. As they went down the hall, the landlady opened her door. "Ah, back so soon, senhor. Did you have a nice walk? Would you like some tea? Come in, come in. How are you feeling? Better?"

"Good evening, senhora." Gaspar stopped and tipped his hat to Senhora Figueiredo, who was flustered and excited to the point she had forgotten to say good evening. "I'm fine, thank you. *Boa tarde.*"

"*Boa tarde*, senhor."

Gaspar and Miguel continued down the hall.

"*Pobrezinho*, you poor man, you should make some friends," Senhora Figueiredo continued. "It is not right that you should be alone."

"I am never alone, senhora."

NIGHT MAGIC

Senhora Figueiredo clearly mistook his words, for she touched the crucifix on her breasts and sighed with deep reverence.

Gaspar smiled and waved good-bye. They entered his room and sat down at the table by the window. They stared out at the night.

"Do you miss the United States, *amigo*?"

"No, not really," Gaspar said. Miguel looked up at him. "I remember, Miguel, and that is enough."

Gaspar lit a cigarette and sat back in his chair. Miguel continued to gaze at the stars through the window. The two made quite a contrast with one another, Gaspar, tall and thin, with wavy gray hair, and Miguel, short, stocky, with straight, dark hair and thick muscular arms.

They sat, silently taking in the night, listening to quiet music on the radio. The sound of the planet spinning, the sounds of restless life on the island, the sounds of the ocean. A voice singing a plaintive note, drifting across the starlit night from afar, or welling up from the deepest depths of the sea.

∼ ∼ ∼

Gaspar Henriques knew plenty about disappearing. Over the years he had vanished so often, it had become second nature to him—at first unwittingly, without foresight or planning, the realization coming after the fact. Like a light switched on and off, it just happened. He might walk into a restaurant or office building unaware that he was invisible, watching people walk right past without seeing him, speaking but getting no response in return. Or he might enter to find all eyes fixed on him, as if he were a ghost who had suddenly materialized in their midst.

He began to practice and perfect the art of fading in and out, willing himself invisible.

Whenever he had left his home in Los Angeles, it seemed the city scrambled like mad, changing what had once been there, altering the landscape to fill the gaps his absence created—as though the city wanted to eliminate all traces of him, to make him a stranger in his own city. Or perhaps he never truly belonged. It was this that contributed to the feeling that he was sometimes being pushed or pulled along, called to other places.

Once his children had grown, his wife removed herself from his life and quietly disappeared.

Gaspar found himself wandering from place to place in search of something that eluded him, some distant or buried memory, a vague forgotten notion of himself.

When he finally returned to Los Angeles, to settle down for what he thought was for good, he began to suspect that bits of him had been left all over the world. Every place and every person he'd come close to, all the people he had known, had kept some piece of him, and now there was little left.

Over the years the message became louder, more insistent, if not clearer. He was a man who had left something behind, and he was now being called back. He'd lived too long in the wrong place, too long in the wrong time; that other time and place were calling him, pulling him, retrieving him.

~ ~ ~

Gaspar Henriques sat in the graveyard with Mariana. She was shy but very fond of him, and even the silence which often hung in the air somehow seemed to connect the two, not coming between them or making those moments awkward in any way, but often making for an understanding that went beyond the need for words or touch.

Gaspar didn't stop to think whether it was crazy for him to be falling in love with the dead girl, a woman who had died a hundred years earlier. Still, he was certain that time, with all its peculiar convolutions, gave one deceptive glimpses of how past, present, and future formed strange geometric designs which allowed him on occasion to view two or more, the here and now as well as the past and present, at the same moment.

Though he never spoke of his feelings, they were inseparable from his words, his posture and gestures, his tone of voice, and above all the radiance that gleamed from his blue eye.

"What did you like to do," Gaspar asked, "when you were still alive?"

"I loved to dance," Mariana said. "There was nothing I loved more in life."

"Were you married, Mariana?" The woman lowered her head.

"No. I died too young to find love. And, besides, I was so devoted to dance. And you?"

"Well, I thought so at the time. However it proved to be a disaster. For years I never had the time. At first having a family, then later always moving, traveling. When I settled down again I lived mostly in books, my work at the library, doing research."

"That is a shame," she said. "I believe you would make a good husband."

Gaspar blushed. "Thank you. You are kind."

"Do you miss your family?"

"Strangely enough, not really. They have their own families now. We are worlds apart in many ways. It's been a long while since I've talked to them. And, when we do, we find we have nothing to say to one another."

Gaspar loved nothing more than to talk with Mariana and hear her sing. Her words buoyed him whenever she told him about her life, her family. Her presence was a current that electrified the night as well as him.

"Why couldn't we have met when you were alive?"

"You weren't born yet," she said quietly.

He laughed. "Are you embarrassed because I'm a younger man?" he asked. "It's okay, Mariana, for you haven't aged a day since your death, remember?"

She smiled, nodded. "In our time you are still as young as ever."

Mariana sang quietly, hushed words of bittersweet love, of parted lovers, of sorrow-filled lives and unfulfilled dreams, the haunting melodies and lyrics of the *fados*. She sang beautifully. And as she sang the wind swept up tiny fragments of tender partings, of early deaths, of steep, cobbled streets and ports of call in distant lands, of loved ones sailing in the crowded holds of ships, of longing, intense undying longing and streams of tears.

Gaspar closed his eyes and listened, the fragments blowing about like leaves playing in the wind around his feet. And in this place of cold gravestones and lifeless, silent tombs, her voice and her words carried him away. Even after the song had ended and the last words trailed off, the thread of life connecting them was forever altered and strengthened.

"Do you believe in life after death?" she said.

"I believe in anything that keeps love and the miracle of life alive."

∼ ∼ ∼

Gaspar Henriques had in a way withered. It seemed at first that life was losing hold of him, the ground pulling him closer. That feeling had steadily grown.

He had moved quickly through the world, unconscious of time, sound, or distance. At each stop he had made, with each person he had dared come close to, he felt himself slipping out from under his own two feet, as though he would fade away or sink into the ground. He moved to keep himself intact. But as he grew older, he slowed, and felt the increasing weight, the source of which he couldn't name, push down on him until he knew he could go no more.

Gone were those times when he could strip his clothes off and work his body flat and wide, concentrating until it truly looked like a sail, or a parachute, and from a treetop or roof he could fall without falling, gliding down as he held his flattened arms and legs out to catch the winds.

Now he felt heavy, leaden. He had become magnetized; he felt the tug and pull of the earth's center. He could no longer run from that. The earth called to him, louder, more insistent. It called to reclaim him—until he found the cemetery at Quebrado do Caminho.

He explained it at first as the effects of some sickness. After all, he had grown very thin. But then there was the fact that while, on the physical level he had slowed, had weakened, at the same time he had come here—to this graveyard on Pico—in a blink of an eye, as if some gravitational force or powerful magnetism had pulled him on a string, bending its own rules of physics to do so. He felt less himself and yet somehow more himself, and also changed, a man caught in two worlds at the same time. But for what purpose?

~ ~ ~

"How is the island doing?" Miguel asked, his voice like the hum of a thousand singing insects.

"It is still working its way to the surface, slowly, but steadily, I believe. Did I ever show you my scrapbook?" Of course he had, many times, but Miguel asked to see it nonetheless. Gaspar pulled the book from the low shelf near his chair and opened it. Aside from the table, the chairs, and the shelf, there was only a bed and nightstand in the room. Gaspar had asked Senhora Figueiredo to remove all the other furniture when he had moved in.

The book was a treasure trove. There were pictures of the island off Capelinhos, in Faial, and a list of the earthquakes and volcanic eruptions that had occurred on the islands over the centuries. There were numerous clippings of newspaper and magazine articles, with dates and locations, as well as pictures of ruined buildings, notations concerning the explosion in 1444 of the mountainside on São Miguel that resulted in Sete Cidades, as well as the 1563 eruption, which created the Lagoa do Fogo, an eerie region of bleak inhospitable landscapes, of icy cold winds and clouds clinging to the mountaintops, where mists shroud the surface of the lake more often than not.

There were notes about the 1620 eruption of Lake Barrenta, in São Miguel, which spewed rocks and ash for several days over a wide area. In Terceira an eruption occurred on July 3, 1638, offshore at Ponta do Queimado, forming an island which then slowly disappeared. In December of 1720, an eruption between the islands of São Miguel and Terceira formed an island about the size of Corvo. It remained until 1723, when it subsided beneath the surface. It is identified on sea charts as the banks of Dom João de Castro.

"I have always been fascinated by the sea around these islands. As you can see, I have studied the activities quite carefully."

"It is a magnificent scrapbook," Miguel said.

"Yes, but they are only pictures, of events long past. I, however, want to see below the surface, I want to find what is happening now, what will be."

"But is that possible, senhor?"

"The world insists it isn't, my friend."

"There is much we cannot know."

Gaspar leaned over and turned on the radio.

"Perhaps the radio will say something about a new island," Miguel said.

"The trouble with knowing or learning about anything," Gaspar said, "is of course a matter of the limitations of the source of the information which you are looking for."

With the droning buzz of the warm air drifting in through the window, and the hum of the radio, Gaspar dreamed. He dreamed of the heat of summer, the oppressive atmosphere, the restraints of rules imposed by a world set upon imposing limitations and restrictions. Even the clothes he wore seemed to hold him back.

He remembered the dizzying restraint of the city, smothered by the asphalt and the concrete, where the force of gravity kept even dreams at ground level.

He yearned to dive beneath the waves, to stay on the bottom and swim with the creatures of the sea, to climb to the top of Pico and blow the clouds from his face. He sought refuge when and where he could, but such havens were painfully inadequate, as well as far and few between: listening to the lowing of the nearby cows, the bleating of the goats, the chirps of crickets; smelling the wild roses and lilac blooming.

Even then he wrestled with the discoveries he made, seeing and doing things his friends could neither see nor do. He felt at ease in the water, going farther and deeper with each new venture; finding a secret spring in the hills where time did somersaults; climbing the heights of Pico as well as the mountains of São Jorge and knowing them to be hollow, connected to one another by subterranean caverns and tunnels, connected to deeper secret chambers below the sea, where legends of the past slept and dwelt, awaiting the moment when they would reappear, rising from the past.

He remembered tapping out signals with a rock upon the mountains, a message to its silent, shy inhabitants; crawling once upon a ledge of rock above Sete Cidades and, for a few brief seconds, floating above the ground, above the mountain and the depths below; lying awake at night, thinking of the mysterious mist-enshrouded girl who waited for him, who promised to be his, sending her powerful telepathic messages, punctuated with countless I-love-yous.

The nights awoke new senses, and he sometimes sat trembling in his bed, tempted to sneak outside, but at the same time fearful of finding what he was sure would be there waiting, things of shadow and of light, gaping bottomless depths, things from the edge of death, the terrifying traps of unleashed imagination.

There were countless things hidden, but real nonetheless. He saw proof of it every day: the muffled cries beneath the black shrouds of frozen lava, drowned out by the crashing sea. The strange language of the *cagarras*, the roar of the wind, the songs which floated like mists across the water, wind and rain that lashed with unleashed fury against the tiny islands, sweeping away roofs, stone walls, trees, sheep and goats. There was the sound you could hear in the *mistérios*, those long frozen tubes of lava, or the small craters on the sides of the mountains, where wind sometimes blew up from the very center of the earth, or the far-off sound of water and an echo whispering, "None of this is real." He shuddered to think of the possibilities. Was he really seeing things—things others couldn't—or was he creating it all himself?

He stayed in bed several days, feeling if not sick, at least different, shedding old skins, becoming a new him beneath a new skin. His room was the universe, and nothing lay beyond. It felt better that way. He tossed and turned on the rough seas of his blankets, crawled across frozen wastes on the ice floes of his sheets, and roamed through dizzying heights of space.

There he studied the surfaces of the moon and Mars.

"Powers of the mind," he whispered shutting his eyes tightly. "Concentration." There he pondered all the imponderables, and always, he felt, the answers, the solutions, just beyond his reach, as if his senses interfered with his ability to comprehend.

He suspected that certain things never happened until they were thought of or dreamt, that imperceptibly he was creating the world as he imagined it, recognizing how it should be or could be, what was hidden behind the veils of reality: what was real, what was not. He quietly wondered whether there weren't some special laws of limitations that governed and maintained the status quo, and if so, how he had managed to invert them.

∼ ∼ ∼

"Listen, Miguel, you know what you missed now?" Rosa said, bubbling over with excitement, as she read the newspaper Gaspar had brought to the cemetery.

Gaspar had come to have a picnic with his friends. The day was a fine one, the weather clear and warm; there was a peacefulness which seemed to emanate from the ground itself, and that even affected the slight breeze that had arisen, playfully stirring a few leaves here and there, but which now seemed to find the task too much an effort, and left the scattered leaves to lay still.

"No, and I don't care to hear," Miguel answered.

"There was a will discovered, from an aunt or uncle of yours who passed away, leaving you a whole mountainside of fertile land."

"Thank you, dear wife. I need this woman hounding me, telling me every day what I missed! Ah, *meu Deus*! Yesterday it was the running of the bulls where five people were trampled to death; the day before that a new book of poetry by a favorite author; and before that a lottery. I swear, if only my bones weren't buried here, I would go find another cemetery where perhaps I could finally get some peace."

Everyone laughed, but they knew better than to believe Miguel's words, for he alone was able to leave the cemetery, for reasons which the others could only guess, assuming it had something to do with Gaspar Henriques.

"Where have you been lately?" Jaime asked Gaspar.

"Oh, I have been staying home listening to the radio for news on the island and watching the papers. They are saying that very soon it may break through the surface."

"An island from the bottom of the sea. It is hard to imagine."

"But imagine is what we must do. People have imagined finding islands for centuries, and many have gone out to search for them, sometimes finding them, only to return again and find nothing, and many have never been seen or heard from again. Perhaps this new island is simply the sea spitting up again what it had once swallowed."

The ghosts watched him, his voice tremulous and eyes closed, the expression on his face hauntingly similar to their own when they recollected, in fond remembrance, the joyous pains of living.

"The birth of a new island," Gaspar went on, "is the birth of new life, new possibilities, the unlocking of secrets deep in the earth."

"It is almost as though it is a part of you, as if you have seen it."

"I have been there, Miguel, at night, in my dreams."

"It sounds heavenly," Mariana said.

Miguel later assisted Gaspar back to his room, after seeing that Gaspar's eyes were getting worse.

"I don't know why, Miguel, but some things I see so clearly, and others—well, it's good to have you here beside me."

"It is my pleasure, Senhor Gaspar. After all, this is the only way I can get away from that bothersome woman of mine."

"Ah, you two couldn't possibly get along without one another," Gaspar said, laughing.

Gaspar listened to the news reports while Miguel gazed at the wall charts of the islands, where Gaspar had marked the location of the eruptions. Then Miguel picked up a book by Fernando Pessoa and read for Gaspar, who sat staring out the window at the Azorean sky above and the sea below, reflecting on how, of late, with the worsening of his vision, came a sharper, clearer, brighter and more colorful sight of his friends in the graveyard, of his view of the island which wasn't yet.

Gaspar realized that, at some point in his life, he had stopped living according to the restraints and parameters that others had imposed upon themselves and the world, that somehow, unconsciously, he had defined his own world.

It was very subtle—but also obvious, he thought, after backtracking through the accumulated years of his life, the events and circumstances which had brought him at that particular time, to this particular place, thinking those very thoughts.

~ ~ ~

Gaspar sat in the late afternoon warmth of the graveyard. The others had left him alone with Mariana dos Reis. Miguel was unsure about the situation and spoke his doubts.

"What are you troubling about?" Rosa said.

"I just think this might not be so good," Miguel said. "A dead woman might take his life, or he might take her . . . ah, I don't know."

"Of course not. Just let the two of them alone. They are lonely. I should know. I could tell you a thing or two about loneliness."

Gaspar and Mariana quietly chatted as he pictured her invisible beauty, the young lady who had died with a heart that had never known love, and whose heart now went out to this man, unlike any she had ever met.

She too dreamed, content and happy when he was there with her, yet insecure at times about the meaning and the unknown ramifications of this love that crossed the lines of life and death, and that so confused her.

Neither was aware of the secret language that electrified the atmosphere surrounding them; nor of the music that somehow arose from the very soil, the trees, the wings of the birds and butterflies that hovered and danced about in the air. "I love you," the sea in the distance murmured. "I love you too," said the wind through the grass. "I've never known anyone like you," the music sweetly whispered. "I'm so happy I've found you," answered the trees in unison.

Their union was reflected in the brushing of branches, in the humming of insects, the joyous chirping of the birds, and in the silent stirrings of the earth beneath their feet. Love was painted across the sky with the dispersion of sunlight and clouds over a pastel blue.

Mariana forgot her earlier conversation with Rosa. "Never mind your pretty head about it," Rosa had told her. "Love is love, and it certainly does nobody any good to worry themselves about it."

"I hope you are right, Rosa. But what can I give him? Not even the warmth of my flesh."

"No, but that is no matter. You have his heart and that's all that counts. To him it is as if you are many miles away, but so much the better for you. He cannot forget about you because you are here with him all the time. It is the perfect arrangement, believe me. I should have been so lucky with my Miguel."

"Oh, everybody knows you two secretly love each other."

Gaspar reached out to touch Mariana's hair, but of course there was no possibility of his feeling her skin or her hair. Even still, when he did, she turned to him as though sensing his touch and she smiled. Her smile in turn warmed Gaspar more than any touch was possible.

∽∽∽

Gaspar stared hard into the dark, the unknown. What was there? What lay beyond sight, beyond the shadows? There was more, much more; he could feel it. Like the invisible matter that littered the unlit regions of the universe, there was so much more that lay beyond comprehension.

How far could he see, with eyes open wide, what was the range and scope of one's vision?

∽∽∽

"Thousands of people die every day," Gaspar said to Miguel. "But very few people's lives, much less their deaths, affect the world. When so many leave and come into the world every day—it makes no difference really."

"But to ourselves."

"Yes. To us we are everything. I don't know if it's better or worse, but those few who are nothing are generally the ones who accomplish the most and are remembered."

"Who are nothing?"

"Who have something—music, some civic cause, art, religion—that takes the place of themselves, that takes away the idea that there are limits."

Gaspar picked things up from the air, the scent of a breeze, the murmuring of the trees, and the chatter of running water. He didn't need to check calendars for upcoming events: no one had to tell him when the weather would change or when the earth would shake and rattle.

Gaspar was physically aware of the inevitability of events that would occur, no matter their distance.

It wasn't even a conscious thought that had driven him to dress up and bring flowers and a bottle of wine to the cemetery for the festival of All Saint's Day, where he first met Mariana, Miguel, and the others. They greeted him like an old friend when he arrived, knowing he was unlike the others who came to pay their respects.

∽∽∽

It had been several days since anyone in the cemetery had seen Gaspar. Miguel finally went to check on him. Gaspar was gone. Miguel followed Senhora

Figueiredo to the hospital. His eyes had gone from bad to worse, leaving him completely blind now.

"Are you stronger, senhor?" Miguel asked.

"It's too early to tell, Miguel. I'll let you know."

Miguel visited him over the next few days, after Gaspar was taken back to his home. Miguel sat and listened to the radio.

"Why is this island so important for you?" Miguel asked.

"It is a new place, a place of myths born of the past but created in the future; the new island, Miguel, like life, is defying death, denying limitations. We can stay here and never move, never dream or think, or we can reach forward, step across the abyss to a new shore. I can't help but believe that somehow this transformation, this leap, will teach us how to survive."

For a moment Gaspar was back in his bedroom as a child. The room was dark, and he was alone. He saw there were worse things than death; he saw the prolific and prolonged death-in-life, in which one became a mere entity, going through the motions but by no means living life, not as it was meant to be lived.

He focused his eyes on the unlit candles on the table in front of him. *Burn* he thought, *burn*. He stared, thinking that one thought again and again, mouthing the words, practicing what he knew he would eventually learn, tasting the sulfur and the sodium nitrate which would one day erupt into the conflagration he so strongly desired.

He lit matches to burn his fingers with, to test himself, in order to withstand the pain; he carefully folded pieces of paper and sailed them out the window of his bedroom, bending his will to keep them aloft, carried farther and farther by the winds his mind conjured, everything practice for the greater leaps he would later make.

∼ ∼ ∼

The radio played softly. The night was warm, heavy with the threat of rain.

Gaspar listened both to the music and for the sound of the skies splitting open. Rain had been falling for two days, a torrential downpour.

He listened to the rain falling again. Looking out upon the darkness from within his own night, he saw the flooded ground erupt with new life, as the barren rocky stretches of land began crawling with green shoots and vines.

Delicate strains of Mozart then, soon after, Tchaikovsky seemed to mimic the instant growth of trees and flowering shrubs.

The rain fell unrelentingly, forming deepening pools and rushing rivulets, which grew into streams, as empty fields suddenly teemed with dense forests.

Gaspar glanced in the direction of the graveyard, his eyes suddenly alive with colors and shapes. The cemetery bloomed with vegetation. And his friends? Were they now embodied as trees, or vines? How many times had the surrounding earth been spilt with blood? The lives of men, women, and children run into the ground. Even animals. How many animals over the centuries had returned their elements to the soil?

And now, right here, every life which had ever touched this ground was being resurrected in plant form. And it was spreading. For where was there a bare patch of earth? A place where blood had not at some time been spilled, and spilled again? Didn't all life, in fact, contribute something in part to the future?

The rain (was it really rain, or tears, or perhaps blood?) continued to fall, breathing new life into the leaves, limbs, roots, and buds of the garden, which rose along slope after slope, spreading into canyons, down riverbeds, and across fields.

Gaspar remembered, many years before, traveling down roads that shot in a straight line to the horizon, through miles without cities or towns. There had been occasional isolated crosses where hardships—perhaps greed or accident—had taken the lives of some traveler, left here and there to enrich a patch of earthen poverty.

∽ ∽ ∽

Miguel came shouting. "Senhor Gaspar, senhor!" Gaspar rose to greet him. They danced with merriment. "What is happening, senhor?"

"I don't know, Miguel. But isn't it wonderful? The earth will be covered with trees. The whole planet, like the garden of Eden."

"And look, senhor, you can see and walk."

"Yes!"

"But how is it possible?"

"I honestly don't know."

"It is a miracle, senhor."

"Yes, yes it is. Where is Mariana, Miguel?"

"I will take you to her. She is back with the others."

Mariana sat waiting, and when Miguel came with Gaspar she stood staring in disbelief. "I don't believe it," she said. "You are whole again?"

He took her hand and they twirled together. "It's true, Mariana! It's true!"

How it had happened he didn't know, but somehow he had broken through yet another barrier, as if he was no longer human, but not dead either, some other stage altogether. A foot in each world.

"I can feel your hand, Mariana!" he shouted.

"I, too, can feel your touch, Gaspar."

Not only had Gaspar changed, but everything else had as well: the island, the cemetery, the air, Mariana. Somehow she too had become more.

They laughed and sang, strolled together arm in arm, as if they were alone in the universe, which was now a garden that stretched on forever, in all directions.

The rain did not disturb them. It inundated the land around them, forming quick rivulets and pools.

Mariana and Gaspar walked and sensed the newfound physicality of their world, listening to birds sing, the happy sound of plants reaching new heights, intertwining and mingling, covering the landscape and filling the air with their scent. Plants with the infinite faces of life.

For the first time Mariana and Gaspar kissed.

The current grew stronger and surged through Gaspar like a halo, and when he touched Mariana it grew and enveloped her as well. She felt it, lifting and pulsing, feeling, as if for the first time: the warm rain pouring; the fire-dance of touch when Gaspar held her or kissed her; the giving and taking without restrain or reservation, but with a free willingness and the desperation that came of the mistrust that there might never be another chance. Miracles didn't often repeat themselves.

Somehow things had become inverted: the more he died, the closer he got to death, the more alive he became, the more he felt.

"I've been a fool. A fool, Mariana."

"But how, why?" she asked.

"Because I'd forgotten where all that power came from. What was its source?" He held her, kissed her. "Now I know."

~ ~ ~

Gaspar waited impatiently for changes to occur with the same eager anticipation of a child awaiting Christmas. When they did, they came about too slowly, in steps too painfully small. Sometimes he waited for years and years while envisioning each new alteration in the universe and how everything would turn out when all was said and done. Why not stay awake all night? Sleep was a thief, stealing valuable time to think and act, to create and seek—until, at last he reconciled himself with sleep, taking into account the fertile potential of dreams. Still, he grew to resent any and all hurdles; even eating seemed a bothersome chore, unproductive and all too frequent an occurrence.

Later Gaspar went back to see Mariana. "Don't go, not again," she said. "It has taken so long for us to find one another."

"I won't go," he said, and they walked, exploring the new richness of a life neither had known before, where the intangible became suddenly tangible, transparent became opaque, and the opaque became light. Where dreams became reality, and reality was anything at all.

No, there was no reason ever to leave now. Gaspar and Mariana ventured farther into the world of their making.

"Life," Gaspar said, laughing.

"Death," Mariana shouted.

"Isn't it all preposterous?"

"It is very silly," Mariana said.

Quebrado do Caminho and the graveyard were a million miles away, and time—no more than a vague uncertainty that the two of them had left behind somewhere, forgotten.

They held hands and walked without really knowing if they were lost in a legion of trees and valleys, rivers and hills which were only illusions, or if Mariana and Gaspar were the illusions. But neither of them thought it mattered.

"Where is Miguel?" Mariana asked.

"He's still back there at my home, I think, listening to the radio. Seems funny, a dead man, worrying himself about news reports of an island being born."

The latest report had detailed how the island, just as it appeared to be on the verge of surfacing, had sunk.

"You are disappointed about the island?" Mariana asked.

"Yes. I had envisioned a new world there, the transformation of a desert into a beautiful place with gardens and water."

"Like here?" she said. "This is so beautiful, Gaspar."

"Yes, it is."

Maybe they belonged here after all. Would they eventually become two trees, limbs intertwined? Would they cover the earth with their vines and flowers, overpowering the rocks?

Gaspar wondered if it could really last, or if it would dry up the way many of the riverbeds did in summer.

She heard the shout before he did. "Senhor! Senhor!" Miguel was looking for them.

He arrived breathless. "It is there, Senhor Gaspar, the island."

"What do you mean?"

"It has finally risen from the sea. The island is there."

"Will you go there?" Mariana asked.

"I don't know. If I do, I may not be able to come back. There are limits."

"I'll go with you," Mariana said.

"And I too," said Miguel.

"All of us together on the new island?" Gaspar said. "Are you sure?"

"You said we can turn it into a garden like here. Why not there too?"

"Maybe we can. What if we cannot return?"

"That is okay. It will be our new home."

"But it has never been done before."

"No, but with you we will do it," Mariana said, defiantly.

Gaspar tried to reason things out, but found he couldn't hold onto anything. Night and time had become a cool liquid. Thoughts slipped away like a thing he tried too hard to cling to. During his last visit to the hospital, the doctors had told him he might lose his other leg. He didn't know if he were more alive or closer to death—or beyond death. It was as if none of that pertained to him anymore.

∼∼∼

As expected, Rosa made a big commotion. "So, you will abandon your wife, an old woman, to go chasing some foolish island in the ocean?"

"I told you we will all be there. Senhor Gaspar, too. An island which will be all ours."

"I refuse to leave. This is holy ground. That new island is not."

"So, we'll make it holy, then."

"But this is our home, where we are buried and where I will stay, alone if I must."

"*Minha esposa*," Miguel said.

"This is how you treat the woman who has loved you beyond death?" Rosa knew she could no more keep Miguel from going than she could keep him from gambling or the wine he liked so much when he was alive. "Go on," she said. "Go chase your new island."

"I will miss you," Miguel said as they parted. Rosa made a sound of disbelief, but everyone knew she was sad to see Miguel go and would miss him very much.

∼ ∼ ∼

Gaspar and Mariana watched the sunset from the new island. "We did it," Gaspar said.

"I'm glad we came," Mariana said.

"Me too."

Miguel was out looking over the strange island, with his wife, Rosa, leaving the two lovers to themselves.

"I told you she would come," Mariana said. "I am happy for Miguel."

"Yes. Those two are full of surprises. I couldn't have done it alone. It's hard to believe we are actually here." He gazed out over the landscape. "It won't look like this for long."

"Will it be beautiful like it was back home?"

"I think so, but it may take a little time. The soil must be developed; it may be quite different. It will be nice to see."

Already the transformation was beginning to take place. The atmosphere around the island drew clouds and moisture, tiny plants took hold in the soil, and the wind, merely the breath of ghosts, dispersed seeds across the surface.

In time life would blossom and bloom, driven by dreams inspired by the hopes of the dead. They would think up the transformation Gaspar had already begun to make, because Gaspar wouldn't let them forget that the impossible was always just beyond reach.

"It will work, won't it?" Mariana asked.

"Yes, now that it's begun, there is no stopping it—the garden will thrive and spread across the land."

"I still don't understand how it happened."

Night was beginning to fall. "It was love, Mariana." It had taken the love of a dead woman to show him the strength he had, to show him what they were capable of together.

Mariana reached over and took his hand. No one else might ever see the island. From Terceira or São Jorge, there might only be a stretch of empty ocean visible to those who lived and sailed on the sea. But it didn't matter—now that they were there. The island was truly theirs.

"It's a beautiful night, Mariana. I hope others will be as lucky to have what we have."

The full moon shone on the surface of the sea, not in one particular place, but everywhere at one and the same time—a million moons and more urging the waves to gently lap against the shore of the new island.

PORTUGUESE IN THE AMERICAS SERIES

Portuguese-Americans and Contemporary Civic Culture in Massachusetts
Edited by Clyde W. Barrow

Through a Portagee Gate
Charles Reis Felix

In Pursuit of Their Dreams: A History of Azorean Immigration to the United States
Jerry R. Williams

Sixty Acres and a Barn
Alfred Lewis

Da Gama, Cary Grant, and the Election of 1934
Charles Reis Felix

Distant Music
Julian Silva

Representations of the Portuguese in American Literature
Reinaldo Silva

The Holyoke
Frank X. Gaspar

Two Portuguese-American Plays
Paulo A. Pereira and Patricia A. Thomas
Edited by Patricia A. Thomas

Tony: A New England Boyhood
Charles Reis Felix

Community, Culture and The Makings of Identity: Portuguese-Americans Along the Eastern Seaboard
Edited by Kimberly DaCosta Holton and Andrea Klimt

The Undiscovered Island
Darrell Kastin

So Ends This Day: The Portuguese in American Whaling 1765-1927
Donald Warrin

Azorean Identity in Brazil and the United States: Arguments about History, Culture, and Transnational Connections
João Leal
Translated by Wendy Graça

Move Over, Scopes and Other Writings
Julian Silva

The Marriage of the Portuguese (Expanded Edition)
Sam Pereira

Home Is an Island
Alfred Lewis

Land of Milk and Money
Anthony Barcellos